THE ORANGE BLOSSOM

A NOVELLA

REL Print Group, a Hezzie Mae Publication

Duluth, MN.

www.HezzieMae.com

ISBN: 979-8-9997402-2-9

Cover Design: Chani Becker @chanibecker.com

Headshot credit @janecanephotography

THE ORANGE BLOSSOM

A NOVELLA

Jebeh Edmunds

HezzieMae
INDEPENDENT BOOK PUBLISHING

Duluth, MN

Dedication

This book is dedicated to my loving husband,
Andrew Edmunds.

I'm blessed to walk this purposeful life alongside you.

Chapter 1: Joviah

In the blistering stillness of the Liberian heat, where the earth itself whispered "awaken," Joviah stepped into a legacy woven with beauty, burden, and a secret that could unravel everything she had thought she knew.

Nearly a year had passed since the Rice Riots had left forty-one protestors dead and hundreds wounded—a brutal voice of unrest that had shattered the veil of peace. The founding settlers' dream that had once shone brightly in the hearts of freed black colonists who had landed on the shores of Africa's first republic was on the brink of ruin. The country's pulse had beaten to the sound of the African drum; its erratic rhythms and speed were not syncopated. The dancers could not find the right direction and had become panicked. The uneasy tension between the descendants of the indigenous peoples and the descendants of the freed settlers was about to tip into a clash that would lead to generational suffering. Through the bitterness, resentment, and foreign powers looming over the administration like hungry vultures, Europe and the United States had kept a watchful eye with suspicion and desperation to keep Liberia under their influence. At the same time, communist regimes had whispered promises to the current president's ear. Tensions had been building, waiting, watching, wondering which way the Lone Star would fall.

On a still February morning in 1980, an older woman, Ma Eliza, woke up just before dawn to start her day as the famed Orange Vendor woman. She was the most well-known market vendor who sold the best oranges in Monrovia. She lay beside her daughter Kebbeh, who was pregnant. In between morning sickness and the movement of her mother waking up beside her on their bed, she ran to the bathroom to vomit. They lived in an upstairs apartment above Nabil's Mechanic Shop, owned by a Lebanese immigrant.

Before one could hear the Islamic call for morning prayer, Ma Eliza woke, touched the cold concrete floor with her bare feet, and whispered, "This is the day the Lord has made; let us be glad and rejoice in it… and the devil is a damn liar."

That had been her crass motivational prayer to start her day. She had a joy in her step as she tied her favorite blue lappa across her waist, tied her hair in her favorite indigo headtie, and put on a pink ruffled eyelet lace shirt. If she was hailed the best orange vendor woman, she had to look the part.

After making pepper soup for her daughter, she set out with her wares and walked to Bendu Street, the busiest street and marketplace in all of Monrovia. One might ask, how had she earned the accolade of being the most famous woman vendor in Liberia?

It was not just her selling the best oranges, but also her technique. The pomp and circumstance of how she sold her oranges as people all over the city waited to see her perform. Before the performance started, she set up and met all of the vendors around her in her area. She enjoyed talking with her friends, and she was ready to sell the best oranges in Liberia.

Her favorite farmer, Amos, had his orange grove two hours north of the city. He came to her apartment every Sunday after church and picked the oranges that he thought would give her the best profit. The market was filled with handmade wood carvings, ivory goods, fresh produce, and colorful lappa fabrics in every geometric pattern and jewel tone that made the eyes dance in delight. The smell of hot palm oil wafted through plastic jugs while the asphalt radiated heat from the pavement, the only relief a warm oceanic breeze that felt like a blanket as one wiped sweat from the neck with a crisp white handkerchief.

Ma Eliza was ready to show off her skills to her customers. Out of her saddlebag, she pulled out her silver pairing knife with a special pink pearl inlay handle. She took each orange and peeled it with her knife, cutting down every single slice. She cut the top half of the orange so that one could peel it off, and just squeeze the orange juice right into the mouth without missing a drop.

This particular day was different. A wealthy man walked up to Ma Eliza's stand and said, "My wife is pregnant, and she has been craving your particular oranges. She told me that she would crucify me if I didn't get your oranges before I got home."

"Hmm, my man, that will be 3 Dollars US."

"Doggit, for one?!" said the wealthy man.

"Look, my man, that's my price," Ma Eliza said. "I see your car. I know you can buy it."

The wealthy man sucked through his teeth in dissent and paid the woman the price. After her choreographed cutting skills, she gave the man the orange, and he headed home to his wife.

This pattern of the wealthy man bickering with the orange vendor woman continued for another few weeks, as he traveled back and forth from the market to his house. Then, the rich man bartered a price that would insult the vendor woman once and for all.

"Ok, look ma, I'm tired of driving back and forth bringing a small orange to my house for my wife every day. I'll tell you what. I've got the money, let me just buy the rest of your oranges, you can just finish your day ahead of time."

The look of shock hit Ma Eliza's face, and she shouted back to the wealthy man, "No! I'm not selling you my whole bushel of oranges."

"Don't you want the money?" said the wealthy man.

Ma Eliza looked at him crossly and said, "Of course I want the money, but what is my purpose in life then? What is my role for the rest of the world if I give you the rest of my oranges now? What would I do? What would be left of me?"

Ma Eliza's main purpose, God had given her, was to serve her people without fear of who wanted to buy her oranges. The wealthy man left disappointed and drove off without the oranges.

Eleven years later, in a small town in Michigan, the life of Joviah Collins had not been the typical American dream. She worked extremely hard to please her parents with her accomplishments. Despite the incessant teasing of her hard-to-pronounce name or the ignorant white peers in her life in the United States, she still persevered. She had to prove to her family back home that all the sacrifices her parents made and left everything they knew would not be in vain. Beatrice would look at Joviah and share this story with her every year on her birthday. Then she would say, "Happy Birthday, my orange blossom," and kiss her forehead.

Her mother, Beatrice—a woman of high Liberian society, skin like ebony, with a drive so eager to keep up appearances for her naysayers back home—would still be envious and reminded Joviah that God's purpose had been her life's assignment; it would come to her, and she would know when her life's purpose was fulfilled. Every birthday, she shared that story of the orange vendor woman in the market speaking up for herself to the wealthy man who could have changed her life. She often wondered if her mother had been the pregnant woman sending her husband on an errand to fulfill her pregnancy cravings.

Joviah's father, Boikai, was a tall man who had shoulders of granite. He introduced himself in the finest suits from Europe. He did not care that he was living with family in the Midwest. He had to prove to himself that he was a success in his role as bank president. His tough exterior had few cracks of calm and humbleness. One really had to work overtime to get that man to validate his only daughter in her eyes.

On the first day of school in her new city, Joviah Collins was familiar with her routine. She put on a nice white Sunday school dress with matching socks with the pink trim. She had a shiny new backpack with fresh supplies and begged her mother to put on her pink head tie. This fabric crown not only made her feel like Liberian royalty, but it also served as a symbol of her heritage. No white children or white teachers would be tempted to touch her hair that her mother had spent countless hours braiding. Sure, she would be teased by young and old at her new school, but she was ready for the ridicule.

Jovi was prepared for the stares and jeers from her white classmates. Moving to Houghton, Michigan, and recognizing that her family was the only black, albeit African, family in her neighborhood was no surprise to her. She knew what isolation felt like.

She knew what the look of the Boogyman must have felt like when kids would ding-dong ditch. But on the first day, it was like this eleven-year-old full of tenacity was going into battle. This battle was to prove her blackness to herself and to prove her Liberian identity to her teacher and white peers. Prove to everyone around her that she would be the only one who would give you permission to see her on her terms, before you rushed to justify who Joviah was, before you got to know her.

The first day of school ritual had been the same every year. Mom made her favorite breakfast. Mickey Mouse-shaped pancakes with fried plantains on the side. She got dressed, taking off her nylon night cap to protect her braids, which were arranged in an intricate pattern that resembled a lattice math equation on her scalp. While Jovi got dressed, she begged her mom to put the head tie on top of her hair.

"Mommy, please do the head tie," said Jovi.

"Why, Joviah? We should keep this head tie for church or a special occasion," said Beatrice.

"But school is a special occasion, it's the beginning of a new chapter in my education," said Jovi.

Hesitantly, Jovi's mother tied her daughter's hair and took her annual school picture outside their door. Beatrice said that posing her only child every year, gripping the doorknob, was a symbol of opening the door to a new school year.

Joviah walked to her bus stop wearing her maroon Members Only jacket, which had a button that read "You're My Eye of Concern," a gift from her mother. She could feel the stares behind her, to the side of her, and in front of her. This didn't bother her. Jovi knew who she was, and she would be damned if anyone told her otherwise.

She approached the bus driver, who had kind eyes. He smiled and said, "Why don't you look important, young lady?"

Jovi smirked and said, "I know I am."

Kids started to laugh, but Jovi sat down in front, staring straight ahead with a little piece of her heart broken. Her parents had always told her to walk with pride because she was a Liberian girl. They had emigrated to the United States when she was only two years old.

Their abrupt departure from their homeland had not only been for freedom from unlawful persecution, but also because they were trying to leave their secret behind. They had felt that starting over in a foreign land with a handful of expat relatives and friends scattered around the country would provide enough of a support base for them to survive.

While the children disembarked from the bus, Joviah stopped and looked at her new school. Walnut Grove Elementary School was where she would begin the 6th grade. Walnut Grove Elementary was the only school in Houghton, Michigan, attached to the local Middle School. Jovi's parents had never thought for a second that placing Jovi in a predominantly white school would be detrimental to her personal development. Their philosophy had always been this: "You're born black, you will die black, the school is within our boundary, get on the bus and go to school."

"What difference does it make, your skin color and your name won't change the situation that you're in," her father, Boikai, had said. "Do you think these white people at the bank who work for me like who I am? No, but they know that they look to me as their black boss, not their African boss."

"They have a job to do, as do I," said Boikai. "Joviah, be proud of who you are, and don't let anybody tell you differently."

Mrs. Matheson, Jovi's sixth-grade teacher, had trouble not only pronouncing her name on the first day of school but also recognizing her gender. "Hovi? Collins? Is there a Mr. Collins?"

Shyly, Joviah spoke and said, "Um, it's pronounced Joe-veeah, Mrs. Matheson. I'm a Liberian girl."

Mrs. Matheson was a young woman who was expecting a child; her belly was already starting to take over her small, tight frame. The kids in the class started laughing and mocking Jovi's name, saying it in the same way their teacher did.

"Now, class, quiet down, I've never seen a name like this before, this is new to me, sorry, dear," the teacher replied.

While she continued with her attendance, one could see the stares of all the white children behind, in front of, and to the sides of Joviah. They watched her, keeping their eyes fixed on the new black kid in class. Unbothered, Joviah sat up tall and glared back at all of them.

There was an announcement for the teacher to go to the office. She told the class to write an essay about their summer vacation so she could get a feel of who they were as writers. Once she left, the teasing and jeers increased.

"Where's Liberia, anyway?" said Frank O'Dell, the red-headed boy who wore shirts like Howdy Doody, complete with pearl buttons and Wrangler jeans. He looked like a student time-warped from the fifties and placed in the classroom in 1991.

Joviah stood up and went to the front of the class, ready to tell all these students where to go, but she stood composed, confident, and poised.

"Ok, listen up before our teacher gets back," said Joviah. "Joviah is my government name, and my real name is Chief Nina of the Vai tribe in Liberia. I wear my head tie to let you all know that you are in the presence of real royalty. I'm doing research for my people back home to compare our American school to the ones back home. The President of Liberia expects my report after every school year."

With doubt drifting around the classroom like a fog over a still lake just before sunrise, Frank spoke up and said, "No way, you're too young to be a chief."

Joviah, with notebook in hand and pencil ready, said, "Frank O'Dell," as she wrote his name in her notebook.

Frank said, "Hey, why did you write my name in your notebook?"

Jovi said, "So when the President of Liberia asks me who was giving me a hard time in my classroom, I can write down their names, and the soldiers would pay them a visit."

Frank's eyes of shock bulged out of his skull, and the rest of the class laughed. Yes, Jovi was not a chief; she had been named after her father's favorite Aunt Joviah of their Vai tribe. Joviah was proud to use that small fact as a suit of armor to protect her from any racist reason to harm her.

The rest of the students sat in silence. Sara Thompson chimed in, "What should we call you then, Chief Nina or Joviah?"

Sara's concern and confusion were written all over her face, but she didn't want her potential friend to feel unseen.

Joviah said, "You may call me Jovi. When my head tie is on, you may call me 'Chief Nina.' That way, you know I'm working on official Liberian business. When my head tie comes off, you may call me Jovi, then you know I'm doing civilian work."

In unison, there was a hush of 'oh.' The footsteps of Mrs. Matheson approached the door. She saw Jovi in front of the class, and the students were still and quiet, with fear in their eyes, as she was at the front and Jovi was out of her desk.

"Joviah, why are you out of your seat?"

Jovi, quick to answer, said, "I was taking a poll of which one of us went on a road trip this summer, Mrs. Matheson."

Joviah winked at the class, "Ok, who went on a road trip this summer? Raise your hands."

As Jovi watched and pretended to count the twelve hands that went up, Frank O'Dell hesitantly raised his hand, but one could tell by the look in his brown eyes that he was trying hard not to believe her, fearful that some African soldier had his phone number.

Jovi sat down with a smirk on her face, victorious that her new classmates had fallen for her big lie, but also annoyed by the fact that she had to carry a notebook and pencil with her everywhere to keep up with this new introduction. The point was that Joviah did not care; that notebook, where she wrote her poems and thoughts, would shield her for the most part from the ridicule of being 'othered' as opposed to being validated.

Why should Jovi pretend, one might ask? Because she was the only Black girl—an African girl at that—who also sounded American. Still, with a funny-sounding name no one got right the first time—and when they finally did, one could not help but burst into an enthusiastic, 'Hey, you got it right!' The poor white person usually startled and backed away, but Joviah did not care. At least she had earned a brief grace period before having to sheepishly correct the next one.

Jovi was ready, notebook and pencil in hand, with a potential 'threat' to contact her soldiers back home, which, of course, she had no power to do, especially back in 1991. Liberia had been in the middle of a treacherous Civil War. Jovi's fear of being bullied at school was the least of her worries. She could feel her parents' anxiety at home, wondering if their loved ones were okay.

The sun shone on Jovi's face as she gripped all of her old library books. The cover had a little boy drumming with the title *The Liberian Drummer Boy*. She did not care that the cover was half torn. She did not care that the old text had a moldy smell. She loved this book because it gave her a piece of her connection back home. She would stare into the eyes of the Liberian drummer boy on the cover and imagine that boy was her brother. She saw a representation of herself that did not make her feel alone in this homogenous environment. She checked out that book over a dozen times. Each time, she would sneak it out into the playground and read it verbatim. She yearned to learn every detail about her home. At the peculiar age of eleven, her unusual name and being the only brown-skinned girl in her class made her feel more connected to her roots back home than in Michigan.

Jovi sat on the bench during recess every day, reading this old yellow book that was over fifty years old, and memorized all the Liberian counties and holidays. She envisioned herself on the beach in Grand Coastal Mound, where her family came from. She closed her eyes and heard the waves crashing and the voices of her people whispering in her ear, "My child, come back home."

She knew going back home was impossible. The war was escalating, and though her heart yearned to return, she knew it would never be in her family's best interest.

Jovi felt like an outsider looking into this stark new home, where kids in their fall jackets screamed and played four-square, tag, and two-hand touch football, which seemed more fun than what Joviah was doing.

"Oh, look, Brownie is reading that stupid book again," Joey, the brunette with more freckles than the constellations, always went after Joviah. He had a scrawny and short stature, and even the teachers feared him.

Jovi looked up and said, "Please, Joey, I'm not even bothering you. I just want to read in peace."

"Oh yeah, it's your book about your 'Library' country. You're from 'Library.' Go back to where you came from, Brownie."

Jovi got up and said, "Shut up, Peach-face."

Joey took the book, ripped it in half, then shouted, "Mrs. Matheson, Joviah called me a Peach-face," as the false tears started rolling down his face.

Mrs. Matheson came across the playground with her box-blonde hair and the smell of Aqua Net, and asked if it was true.

Jovi said, "Yes, but he keeps calling me Brownie and ripped up my library book."

"Now, Joviah, you know you're not supposed to bring library books outside," said Mrs. Matheson. "You'll have to bring that back to the library and pay the fine for the ripped book. Now go and apologize to Joey. Next time he calls you these names, you need to tell me first."

"Mrs. Matheson, I have. Isn't it weird that he brings brownies to school and shouts in class, 'Look, I'm eating Joviah's relatives,' but you say nothing?"

"Now, Joviah, go to the principal's office for talking back. I don't know what they did in Africa for children who talk back to their teachers."

"There's no talking back to teachers in Africa, because the teachers listen to their students the first time," said Joviah.

Jovi clutched her tattered yellow book as she walked, head down, shame and fear heavy in her chest, tears streaming down her face. She worried about the consequences of what was to become of her, both in school and at home, after the principal had called her parents. *"Mommy will pepper me for true,"* she whispered under her breath.

Grandpa used to say, "Every time a book is destroyed, the author loses a piece of their soul."

The desecration of the story was the sheer amount of disrespect for the author's life's work. Grandpa had told her that when he saw her draw and rip the pages out of her *Cat in the Hat* book. She had cried at four years old, thinking she had just killed a piece of Dr. Seuss. That kind of lecture sticks with an African child for the rest of their lives.

Fourteen years later, in Joviah's New York City apartment, the weight of optics pressed hard. So much damn optics. She wasn't smart enough for Daddy—always a disappointment. Sometimes it felt like he looked at her with nothing but regret for having a daughter.

"Who will carry on my legacy?" It had been the slogan he'd mutter under his breath since she was a toddler. His sheer disappointment that she wasn't born with a penis haunted her.

How could this creative woman carry on the legacy of Boikai Collins? Her mother just ignored him and said that women were the future, but she cringed anytime she tried to stand up to him. Did she not know that she did not protect Jovi? Did she not see that his jokes were the reason why she saw her therapist twice a week?

At least it was his money, so she guessed his legacy was investing in her pain and hurt that he had created all these years. So yeah, she supposed she was really fulfilling his ROI. There she went, drifting off again in her pain, where she should have been sketching her latest capsule collection. She got so angry. Sketching to Sade, even though her music resonated with her soul, brought up a lot of triggering feelings. But her lyrics and Jovi's 'attitude' had her rocking her third New York Fashion Week show in Soho.

"Joviah, where did you put the crockpot?"

"Eh meh, Mommy. You know I need to get my sketches done for the pattern maker."

"Well, if you put it back where I put it, I wouldn't ask you shit. I swear, I can never find anything in this zinc shack of an apartment."

Her mom said that when she came to visit Jovi in New York, she felt like she could go camping. She enjoyed it so much that she refused to rest in Jovi's bed; instead, she laughed and made a pallet on the living room floor. Then she got scared because she swore she saw a rat and jumped back in bed with Jovi.

Mind you, Jovi lived in a kick-ass townhouse in Brooklyn that overlooked the river, and she had bought it herself with her proceeds from her first fashion show. She guessed her mom still loved checking in on her.

She did not think her mother was disappointed in her decision to attend the Fashion Institute of Technology (FIT) right out of high school. Her mother kept saying that Daddy would get over it, but Jovi was 25, and he had yet to visit her. He was pissed because she had turned down a full-ride engineering scholarship to Michigan Tech. Again, he hadn't learned this in the parent handbook—that your dreams don't necessarily translate to your child's dreams.

Her mother used to say, "If you ask a child a question, you must accept the answer."

He asked her, when he found her cutting up dresses in an old JCPenney catalog, what she wanted to be when she grew up. She had told him that she wanted to work in the fashion industry. He took the catalog and chucked it across the room.

He said, "You'll end up selling your clothes on the street." Then he added, "I didn't leave Liberia for you to be making clothes in this country. What am I supposed to tell my friends back home?"

She ran into her closet, clutching her clippings, her face soaked in tears. Her father had been her first critic, the one who had initiated her thick skin. Why did she still want his validation?

The hard work she had done was not enough; her parents refused to pay her tuition to FIT. She worked double shifts at Mario's Pizza in uptown and found a great Korean-owned fabric shop. She quickly learned that if she went in speaking her broken Liberian English, they would give her a discount. She created a bridal fashion line for her senior graduation capsule collection and discovered that she had a passion for designing wedding dresses.

Fast forward, and now she had her own wedding dress line, *Wedding Couture by Jovi.* You knew you had made it big when you saw brides try on your dresses at Kingman's Bridal Boutique.

Her dresses were elegant, fierce, and had a nod to her African roots. Brides came down the hall, looking better than the bride in the movie *Coming to America.* Her dresses averaged between $10,000 and $30,000, but her mother thought she was slumming it when she visited. Jovi swore she tried so hard to prove her worth to her parents, but she was just exhausted.

She loved going to Harlem and just sitting to look at the mural right outside the Apollo Theater. There were two African women; one had her hair wrapped in a yellow and blue head tie, wearing a green dress, and was holding a card, accompanied by African print quilts. Another African woman was looking away in the distance.

This mural was both grounding and motivating. How could she be a high-fashion designer and not have been back home? Why was she so damn obsessed with African textiles, but had never been home to see exactly how these fabrics were made?

She heard the murmurs about being a cultural appropriator, but this was who she was. She was a Liberian woman who had been raised in the United States.

She saw the pity in her relatives' looks, knowing Joviah was trying her hardest to belong. Couldn't her lived experiences also be a part of the Liberian experience? She hadn't gotten the choice to stay behind, yet she should have survivor's guilt for living in America?

Damn, she needed to walk away from her desk. She would show her mom Mario's Pizza for lunch. Yet, she needed to stop putting off this deadline. She needed to sketch five more designs, but nothing was coming to mind at the moment. This was what happened when she tried to create a capsule every year. The vicious cycle of trying to create something new out of thin air, recalling her childhood traumas, Dad's disappointment, visualizing the mural in Harlem, going walkabout in town, having amazing, toe-curling sex, and creating kick-ass designs.

Let's start walking; she had a deadline to meet.

Jovi had met her fateful soulmate on a Saturday at a reggae bar in uptown with her girls two years ago. She had walked in wearing a red scrunched-up strapless dress from Forever 21 and approached a beautiful, dark-haired, sky-blue-eyed white boy at the bar. He wore an American Eagle t-shirt and khakis. She had two dollars to her name and asked if he was lost.

"The grunge garage band bar is six blocks away."

He said he wasn't lost and loved listening to reggae music. Jovi rolled her eyes and said, "Lemme guess, you had a nanny named Matilda in your parents' estate in upstate New York who played Bob Marley while you napped."

He laughed and said, "Nope, I'm Canadian-born from Minneapolis, Minnesota, and we had a radio station every Saturday that played reggae music every Saturday morning. DJ Bongo Terry was the shit."

Jovi nearly spat out her Long Island Iced Tea. Okay—assumptions weren't the best first impression. She asked his name, and he said, "Henry Anderson"—the whitest name she had ever heard. She told him her name was Joviah—Jovi, for short.

She told him she was Liberian but had grown up in the UP of Michigan. They talked the whole time—right up to the bar's last call. Then they took the conversation to her place, and once again, her assumptions were way off. How could one conversation, a worn American Eagle tee, and a night of unexpected reggae connection convince Jovi that she had just met her husband? She wondered what her parents would think about Henry. Would they accept him for who he was? Or would they tell her to find a nice Liberian man to marry?

Boikai met Henry the following year and smiled at Joviah, whispering with a chuckle, "You've been in America too long, mehn, I'm not surprised."

He turned to Henry and said, "Welcome to the family, young man, you have my blessing."

Beatrice, on the other hand, looked at Henry and said, "I wish you both well," before running out of her kitchen with tears in her eyes.

Joviah looked at Henry, surprised, and ran after her mother. Beatrice was sobbing by her bed. Joviah asked her why she was so upset.

Beatrice put her head up and said, "I'm so happy for you that you get to live freely with your future by your side. I envy you, my child."

In that moment, Joviah realized her mother's tears weren't for what she had lost, but for the life she had never been strong or free enough to choose.

Chapter 2: Beatrice

They were anointed the honorable ones: nearly one thousand Black settlers from the Americas and West Indies who escaped lives of degradation and atrocity to find a better way of living, from the promise of humanity they would never receive in their stolen homes. Be that as it may, missionaries, freed slaves, and priests survived disease and weather to start a new life with a blueprint for their free land. Two generations later, the descendants of those survivors created a mass haven of traditional African values and free enterprise. Housed in plantation-style mansions with foundation posts jutting above the deep emerald lagoons, all that separated the lives of the honorable ones from the fray of the countrymen climbing their way to the top.

Joviah always believed her parents' love story was one of tradition and devotion—but the deeper she looked, the more she realized it was woven together by expectation, fear, and ambition. Out of fear of losing the respect of her parents, Beatrice adhered to the tradition of marrying one of their own.

When Beatrice met Boikai Collins, he was boisterous, magnetic—the kind of man who loved attention from women. He studied hard, impressed his professors, and never shied away from showing off his ability to charm anyone effortlessly. Beatrice was intimidated. Boikai stood six feet tall, a true Adonis, and she often felt unworthy of his notice. His charisma was undeniable: eyes like deep pools of oil, a smile that made you feel as though you were meant to enjoy his presence.

Joviah finally understood the meaning of her mother's name: "The blessed one," derived from the Latin Beatrix—she who brings happiness. Beatrice carried the weight of being that light in a family full of absorbers, the pull of despair always lurking. She was the only child of her mother's womb to survive, and the pressure to live as the "blessed one" shaped her every step.

Her mama had difficult pregnancies, and Beatrice was her tenth try and a success. Absorbing her mother's grief for her nine children who did not survive was in her womb. She would comb her hair at night, resting her head on her mother's inner thigh, and hear her mother recite Psalms as she plaited her hair.

Survivor's guilt is a free way of thinking. People who came to Beatrice's house would whisper, "Hmm, Beatrice—oh, you are the light to your parents, oh! They had such a hard time borning a baby, then came you! God is so good, oh!"

It's a wonder how my birth and exultation of greatness that I didn't ask to be has left a birthmark on my left cheek by my ear. Her father would boast that it was the kiss from her angelic siblings. I get so embarrassed by it that I try to cover it up with my long hair. He thinks that I feel shame by it, but I just don't feel the need to explain to people.

It's hard to live at home at seventeen. The constant scrutiny—only seeing friends during the day on Saturday, no beach trips, no riding a bicycle. Her gran said, "Riding bicycles is for fast girls. If I catch you, you will catch a hard time, oh."

The expectations not to run behind boys or go to the beach would catch all getting up.

Their stately home, overlooking the beach, was filled with love, discipline, and respect. Beatrice's friends in Monrovia looked out for each other and got into a little mischief along the way. Beatrice loved sneaking out to the beach to read, clear her head, and reflect on where her life would lead. The ocean was her true sanctuary that she never found at church. The sound of the waves crashing along the shore in such a rhythmic pattern calmed her thoughts and fears. Any major life decision would be made on that beach. She needed the symbiotic sound to ground her back to Earth. The place that was her sanctuary was also the most forbidden to visit.

I was raised to focus solely on my studies; I was expected to bring our family to great expectations of grace and poise. I was taught etiquette classes by Sister Marguerite every Wednesday after my private tutor sessions. I was raised to go to school at home because my parents thought I was too precious to go to school with my friends. Their precious gift couldn't face any danger or influence to do terrible, ungodly things. They would have none of that.

I was a prisoner of influence, reputation, accomplishment, and simplicity. Our daily routine included attending Catholic Mass at St. Mary the Immaculate every Sunday, followed by a fellowship gathering at the parishioners' homes, where I was tasked with serving hot Ovaltine and shortbread biscuits. Mama would be with the women in the parish in the foyer. They would gossip about whose husband was caught on the beach with some woman in the church, who would remain nameless as I passed.

Still, we all knew who they were talking about—Hannah Perkins, that 22-year-old Peace Corps student from Alabama who just wanted to know what it was like to be with an African man. She didn't care if he was married; African men were her conquests on her short 'mission trip' to the motherland to justify her anthropology degree to her white Baptist parents from the Bible Belt.

My father would be in the den playing cards with the men, talking politics, diplomacy, and, of course—the sweet American girl, Hannah. She was "very interested" in our government relations and just so impressed by how advanced African people are in Africa. I was in charge of fetching their Club Beers and cigars. I would pass by these rooms, unassuming, do my duty to fulfill all the adults' needs, and return to my room to play my flute to entertain them.

My father was the Minister of Commerce for Liberia under the Thomas administration. Our compound was lavish—he wanted it to look like a French chateau. My parents were highly regarded for their Liberian and Americo-Liberian heritage. My mother's sister was the maternal aunt of a former Liberian President. My grandmother, Josephine, was the daughter of a wealthy Methodist missionary from Jamaica who came to convert the Indigenous people.

My father was a God-fearing Catholic who valued education and equal rights for women. He wanted me to learn as much as I could—to one day educate the next generation of our children.

Monday through Friday, teachers would come to the house. I studied Latin, French, Calculus, Music, Sewing—and read my Bible. We were studying the book of Joshua. The main theme of Joshua, before he did, he said, "But for me and my household, we will serve the Lord."

It is my duty to serve and to serve my household, because I am the blessed one.

My mother, Geraldine, would say, "The beach is where our people would disappear and never come back."

I knew she meant the area where the slave catchers would take our people, but there were no slave catchers in 1975. My mother was still haunted by this fact and passed down the anxiety of losing someone that she loved on that same beach where our people had been taken before. To her, it was a place of no return. To her, it was a place where it never ended well.

To me, it's where I speak to those ancestors' spirits from the past, and they guide me to where I need to go next. They whisper in my ear and guide my spirit to the next choice in my life.

Yes, stubbornly, I wouldn't listen to their whispers but to my heart, and I hear them say as I return to the same beach, "Welcome back, my child, you have learned well."

I must say, the childhood I had was of privilege and scrutiny; I was the girl in the bright, big house on the hill across from the French embassy. My friend John worked in the US Embassy down the street. He really loved my shortbread biscuits, and I would meet him on Wilson Street to drop off a midday treat. He had red hair and more freckles than the constellations. He seemed to particularly like to chat and play chess with the Marines who were stationed at the embassy.

John was a 20-year-old on assignment with the CIA. He was from Pittsburgh, and you think that those shortbread biscuits were made with gold. John would tell me stories about his life back home. His parents were Jewish, and he liked to watch American football. His team, the Pittsburgh Steelers, was the latest Super Bowl Champions, beating the Minnesota Vikings this year.

I kept asking him, "What kind of bowl? What are they stealing?" He just laughed—his grin was mesmerizing. I wasn't baking those shortbread biscuits just to be polite.

John's eyes were blue like silk, and his red hair was something I'd only seen in my imagination. He said his mother used to get teased—how could a Jewish boy have red hair? They called him the Milkman's baby. His idioms always confused me. Now, I wonder—if that milkman had red hair, maybe he was your Pa.

Aye God, if I do go to America, I will go to Pittsburgh and find Mrs. Horowitz's front porch and watch that milkman to see if it's for real.

Between studies, I'd fantasize about what it would be like to be married to a Jewish-American man. I'd scribble in my notepad: Mrs. Beatrice Horowitz. The next morning, I met John at our usual spot. We walked behind Wilson Street to a side street and held hands, out of sight of anyone. Kids were chasing after dogs on the quiet street, and elder men were playing cards atop a peach crate. The feeling of John and Beatrice strolling together without a care in the world about who saw them holding hands. One of the old men stopped playing his cards to look up and see the couple, with a toothpick hanging from the side of his mouth. He let out a disapproving grunt and kept playing his game.

John smiled at the old man and said, "Grunt all you want, I love this woman."

Beatrice felt the hot sun glowing on her face. She thought, John declared his love for me! In this alleyway?! What would our people say if we got together? People who married outside their race were the butt of jokes in Liberian society in the early 1970s. The notion of a Liberian woman at the time falling in love with a white American man looked like a sign of her own desperation.

Beatrice didn't care what people thought; she loved John so much. They both stopped under the plum tree hanging over a tall white cement fence and kissed. John's lips were soft and thin, but they felt safe. In that moment, the clouds parted, and it started to rain. Beatrice and John looked up and laughed, held each other, and walked sheepishly back to the embassy.

Shoot, my Pa himself would disown me to marry a white man, let alone a Jewish man at that, thought Beatrice. What would those parishioners think on Sunday afternoons? I didn't want to be seen as a disappointment—or the running joke like Hannah Perkins (now Hannah Bomi). You see, there's a town called Bomi Hills, and the neighborhood kids would tease Hannah's children, singing loudly in their best Julie Andrews voice, "The hills are alive with the sound of Bomi."

What! Those kids would fight, oh. I guess Hannah found her African man and had his five light children, but that's not my business. After Sunday service, Hannah's business was all the fodder over hot lemon tea at the house.

Old Ma Perkins would say, "That's what happens when you get a frisky white woman who overstays her welcome."

Old Ma Yancy would say, "Stop it, you know you're frisky too, oh."

The following month, after my French lesson, I walked with a basket of shortbread biscuits and a letter I'd written, confessing my love to my dream Jewish-American. I told him I'd used extra nutmeg in the recipe and hoped we could court—and maybe someday go back to Pittsburgh together.

I went back to Wilson Street at our usual one o'clock, but John wasn't there. I waited an hour.

John never reached me.

Walking back home with my basket in hand, I saw a Marine walking toward the embassy. I knew he was friends with John, and they would talk about football and argue about the Super Bowl. I think he was from Minnesota. He said that John had been reassigned to Paris.

No goodbye. I'd miss his smile, knowing I'd never see those kind eyes again. The Beatrice Horowitz fantasy died that day—with extra nutmeg.

Boikai was in line to get a job working in the Ministry of Commerce & Industry once he graduated. My own father knew from his colleagues that Boikai was the top choice in the field. He could equate economic performance that would lead his country into a sustainable force that all of Africa would see. This 21-year-old man had his plan ahead of him.

Beatrice contemplated why Boikai favored her. Was it her father's coveted position in the government that made her so appealing? Was it her family status that would get him the opportunity he'd worked so hard for?

He then again chose her. I always felt his connection to me was a mere obligation. I was his elevation to status; my name alone gave him access to the movers and shakers in society. Our arrangement was nothing short of an agreement between our families, yet I learned to be his chosen partner.

He always seemed distracted during our conversations. It felt as though he fantasized a different spirit conversing with him instead of mine. He was my second boyfriend, my first lover, and my last hope to leave my family home.

I, too, was distracted in thought. I yearned to fantasize about John's spirit in front of me. I closed my eyes every night and saw John's blue eyes staring back at me, and the curvature of his grin would calm my slumber. John was a forbidden hope of a life together. Boikai was a man of opportunity, and I was it.

I was his last hope to gain the respect and power of our country.

After Sunday mass, I'd listen to the murmurs of my father's friends as they spoke of Boikai. "He will bring economic stability to Liberia." "He will continue your legacy, Papay." "We don't want to deviate from what our forefathers desired."

Five years later, Liberian society was excited to witness the wedding of Boikai Collins and Beatrice Hinton. People were hopeful to get an invitation made from special paper imported from France. All were excited to see the opulence of what their mothers had taken months to plan. Beatrice made a vow to herself before her marital vows. She chose herself in silence. She chose her forbidden love's face every time she slept. She would choose this new life of obligation without love. She accepted the companionship that had created the baby inside her womb as she prepared to walk down the aisle and fulfill the arrangement set forth before her.

Little one, I know there is another being inside another woman. I promise you that 'other' child will come, and I will see to it that being won't spoil your greatness.

Their wedding was published in the Liberian Gazette. There were administration ministers and dignitaries at St. Mary the Immaculate Church—so many that Bishop White told the guards to conceal their weapons in the house of the Lord.

When her father walked her down the aisle and gave her away to Boikai, she saw the look in her betrothed's eyes and felt a chill of caution before she recited her vows.

God told her to look at the back of the church, and there she was: a woman journalist, Kebbeh, in the background with her press badge and notebook in hand, a single tear running down her cheek. She wore an indigo tunic that ever so slightly covered her shape. She placed her right hand over her stomach, breathed deeply, and shook her head at me—mouthing the words, "please, no."

I looked at Boikai—sweat pouring down his face, his bright smile—unaware that I knew his little secret, because I was secretly carrying a child inside me, too.

I smiled at him and recited my vows. After he spoke his, I held his hand and put his hand discreetly on my stomach, and the grin on his face made the angels rejoice. No one was ever going to disrupt this new marriage, so help me God.

As we walked up the aisle after the ceremony—dignitaries and commoners alike—I looked Kebbeh in the eyes, gave her a victorious smirk, and whispered, "Congratulations." Boikai and

Beatrice walked out of the church, their hands gripping a new beginning of betrayal and uncertainty.

Eleven years later, in the United States, the dreams of starting over with Beatrice's family in this new country were both terrifying and exciting. She wanted to make a name for herself. The hope of her family being whole again after months apart ached in her soul. She wanted her daughter Joviah to live in a world where her dreams could become reality—one that didn't come with the baggage of status or a familial past.

She hoped that her husband would end his Playboy persona and finally be the family man he promised her he would be. Even Hannah Perkins knew where her husband Boikai's birthmark was located. The sheer fact of embarrassment was etched on Beatrice's face. Most nights, she felt alone raising their child with only the hired help. She felt the weight of preparing for life with the three of them, with only one person at the helm.

The night before they left for America, Boikai went to work and was at a checkpoint. Rebel soldiers wanted his car. My mother used to say how much he loved his bright blue 1978 Chevy Monte Carlo. There's a picture on the fireplace mantle— baby Joviah frowning, being held across her father's lap, sitting with her dad in front of his dream car. He'd joke that he was in front of his dream car and his dream girl. He loved that car, polishing the rims every Sunday after church. He'd scrub the tires and the whole car, ready to be 'bluffin' in the church parking lot.

Everyone in Monrovia knew Boikai's car. He would even pay a small boy outside his office at the Ministry to watch the car. Her dad would pay that small boy to make sure a bird didn't soil it; the boy would be on constant watch, making sure no one looked inside.

After work, Boikai was stopped at the checkpoint. The soldier asked for his ID and inquired about why he had left his house after curfew.

Boikai said, "Man, I owe you?"—slang for Do I owe you an explanation? In other words, none of your damn business.

The soldier and Boikai started quarreling, and two more soldiers stopped by. The first soldier knew Boikai from childhood church school; he wasn't just a soldier but that strange boy, Foday, who used to tease him for being 'too dry' to eat.

After soldier Foday made Boikai get out of his dream car, Boikai stumbled out when the soldiers surrounded him. Foday said, "With all this damn bluffing around town, Boikai, you're still pushing your damn mouth with your dry self."

Fun fact: When someone calls you "dry," they mean you're skinny as hell—not exactly a compliment.

"This time, I will destroy your car for making me vexed," Foday said.

Boikai was scared; the other soldiers laughed and teased him, wanting Foday to destroy the car in front of the cocky Boikai they'd seen all over town.

"Now, you're acting big shot, eh?" Foday said. "Now, big shot, shall I just shoot you in the street like a Kick-it dog? Or should I just shoot your car?"

"Shoot the bastard," the third soldier yelled.

"He's wasting a long time. Shoot the damn bastard, Foday!"

Boikai begged for mercy. Foday lit a match and held it close to Boikai's face—making the sweat glisten on his terrified skin—then laughed and tossed the match inside the bright blue Monte Carlo, which started to ignite.

Boikai begged and pleaded for his life. He said he could buy a new car, but my wife and child were at home.

"I beg you, Foday, please let me go!"

Foday and his comrades started shooting at the ground near Boikai's feet. They jumped him, took his money from his wallet, and sent him home limping, with tears in his eyes and his dream car engulfed in flames behind him. He was grateful for his life, but he knew this wasn't the life his baby girl deserved.

Three months later, with two plane tickets, Boikai, Beatrice, and baby Joviah saved enough money and boarded a Nigeria Airways flight to JFK Airport in New York City. Boikai said that Joviah was a very busy toddler who cried the whole way. He couldn't imagine she'd be difficult for the entire long journey to the States. Joviah wore a bright yellow lace dress with eyelets sprinkled throughout. Yellow ribbons were in her hair, tied by Aunty Maggie, Beatrice's best friend, who gave Joviah a final kiss on her right cheek goodbye.

Aunty Maggie was shot that evening, protecting her son from a robbery gone wrong. The young couple's mother boarded the plane, switching laps for a restless toddler. Leaving the life they knew behind, undeterred by Joviah's demands for 'fwied plantains' and tears, they both prayed for the rest of the passengers to have grace on the long journey.

Beatrice shared that Joviah never wanted to leave Mama Liberia behind. She knew that day that Joviah's yearning would take a lifetime to return to her beloved homeland.

Once the Collinses arrived in the United States, there was no ticker-tape parade; they landed in a new country, stripped of their Liberian elitist clout, and were baptized as three more Black people on the shores of the land of the free. Luckily, they knew English and met childhood friends at the airport who had been in the States two years prior.

Delvin and Louise Dixon were close to Beatrice back in her neighborhood. Louise often helped Beatrice escape the house of discipline and overreach. At ten, the girls ran on Embassy Row, staring at the Marine Corps barracks. When a Marine guard was at the gate, he would smile and give the girls whistle candy, which made them smile, grab, and run away.

Louise's mom caught the girls with their candy and asked where they got it. Beatrice confessed, and they both got punished for going over to the forbidden Marine zone.

Louise's mom said, "If I hear or catch you on that Embassy Row again, you will really meet the twelve disciples when I'm finnish flogging y'all. Eh-hen?"

Although their bums were sore, they laughed to themselves and joked, "Next time we get caught, which disciple will we meet first in the line, John, Paul, Simon..."

Louise and Delvin had a dry cleaning business in Camden, New Jersey. They loved where they lived and worked very hard.

They were card-carrying Methodists eager to compete to see who was most devoted in the eyes of Christ.

The Collinses stayed in their tiny apartment for a couple of months to plan where their family should settle in their new country. Boikai worked as a bank teller and hated it; despite his extensive experience in Liberia, it didn't translate to promotions. His boss at Eagle Bank didn't know Liberia was a country, let alone where it was.

Beatrice stayed home and worked at a community college, cleaning classrooms, until her University of Liberia transcripts were transferred, allowing her to continue her education in the United States. Although Louise was her mother's childhood friend, Joviah was always directed to call her Aunty Louise—a sign of respect. In Liberian culture, if you call an elder by their first name, it's almost an insult.

What was supposed to be a few months in New Jersey ended up being two years. Beatrice finally got accepted to Michigan Tech. Boikai was also excited to leave New Jersey traffic for Michigan.

They settled in an apartment complex not far from the Michigan campus, built for students who were married with children. Joviah thrived there, with a Head Start right on campus, and Beatrice would drop her off on the way to class. They found a Liberian AME Church twenty minutes away, helping them integrate into the community. Though not related, everyone knew the Collins and Hinton families from back home.

They had cultural capital. The Collins name carried respect in this new community, yet Joviah began to see how respect in

America could feel different—quieter, more fragile than the honor their name had carried back home.

Chapter 3: Boikai

The 1970s in Liberia were a time to rally the youth. The administration deemed their youth as the country's 'precious jewels.' Like diamonds under pressure, the weight of their parents' expectations was insurmountable, urging them to take the baton and reach even farther for the next generation. Caught in a delicate dance, the young people of Liberia balanced their own dreams of independence against the ambitions their parents had prescribed for them.

The Coconut Husk Dance Hall in 1978 was a popular spot on a hot summer night, located just fifteen minutes outside of Monrovia, where the bosses of the city would frequent with their sugar ladies, and a mixture of expats from the US and college coeds would pack in.

The beer flowed, and the polyester pants and hot pants arrived there in every hue. The DJ was the best maestro in the country. The aromatic scents of wild musk oil, sweat, and cigarettes hypnotized the patrons looking for a good time. Wooden chairs were strewn across the parquet floor, and the tables had been stacked against the walls.

No one talked about business or politics. Everyone was there, dancing in joyful rhythm—from disco jazz to Bob Marley's Could You Be Loved to Aretha's Rock Steady. The pulsating sound made the bass feel through the body, and the soul sang with every song. The energy of dancing and moving their bodies to the sound seemed to seek a way to escape.

The music was Boikai's escape. Escape from the pressure of society. Escape from the pressures of his father. Escape from the stress of his new position in government. There, he was a somebody without the spotlight of expectations that would blast him each morning. He could enjoy his Club Beer with friends without having to explain his absence to his fiancée. Beatrice was too sophisticated for a place like the hall. It would be unheard of to patronize the fringes of society. Those people were an arm's length away from total exile. In contrast, at the concrete bar—its green checkered blocks scarred with cigarette burns from drunken games of tic-tac-toe—Boikai's friends eagerly awaited, ready to welcome him back to the motherland.

"Look who's back, a 'been to,' eh," Richleau Martin said as Boikai entered the dance hall. ("Been to" was a term for Liberian youth whose affluent parents sent them abroad to study in the U.S. or Europe—a way of saying, "You've been to America, so you think you're better than us who never left.")

The teasing didn't break Boikai's spirit. He endured far worse going to Covington Episcopal School in Connecticut. It was brutal being a young Black African boy in the '60s and '70s with a name that had "boy" in it. The racist whispers—calling him a "Monkey eater"—and the casual use of "boy" by white classmates happened anytime Headmaster Calhoun wasn't around.

"Been to" didn't faze him. But the cruel pranks—like his bunkmate urinating on his school clothes in his dresser—stuck with him well into adulthood. Boikai frantically washed his urine-soaked uniforms with the Ivory soap flakes his mother sent, determined that as an "eye in a blind man's town," he would be the bravest eye the world would see.

The old adage of knowing he would be the only Black body in the presence of white society held true. The expectation to prove his worth and presence without backing down in a fight was relentless. Boikai was determined not to let his tormentors block him from the assignment his father had spoken about the day before he entered Covington, his ninth-grade year.

His father said, "I did my research, and Covington has the most prominent children of US government and diplomatic leaders."

His father was one of the key leaders in the Liberian Shipping Registration Company. He and a few colleagues were responsible for registering cargo and passenger ships that sailed the oceans. After World War II, ships would save hefty money on labor unions. If a US ship needed to hire an all-American crew to have Old Glory flanked on the ship's body, Uncle Sam could keep more of his coffers by purchasing those fees at a minimal price through Liberian registration—a cosigner using the Liberian flag of convenience to steer clear of US labor laws, the ultimate capitalist loophole.

Boikai was instructed to form relationships with high-profile students at Covington to strengthen US-Liberian diplomatic and commercial relationships upon graduation. Although the pressure was high, Boikai yearned for friendships that were beyond an assignment. He felt lonely in his dormitory, waiting patiently for holidays to reunite with his family back home, if only to escape the hurt and harassment at school.

Boikai had always been a very introverted boy. Yet his twin brother, Boima, didn't speak until he was five years old. Their mother, Sandra, prayed for a miracle. She made sure that when Boikai visited on holiday, his favorite grapefruit was cut open, the flesh dug out on a small saucer, filled with Carnation evaporated milk, returned to the rind, sprinkled with sugar, and served with Ovaltine.

Their home was the color of red clay, with wrought-iron bars covering the windows and beautiful, floral cut-out cinder blocks on top of a hill overlooking the ocean. The Collins brothers were often compared to stir up friendly competition. Boima was indeed gifted. Boikai thought Boima waited to speak until he was five because he was memorizing everyone's conversation.

After church, the Collins family always upheld their sacred ritual: breaking the fast only after communion. Boikai Senior, powerful and commanding, made it law. Once the body of Christ was shared, their dining room overflowed with soups, stews, fruit, and fellowship. Guests came hungry for food, but also for the spectacle—where ridicule sat as freely at the table as the dishes themselves.

On one unforgettable Christmas, Boikai Junior became the spotlight of his father's cruelty. After his fourth helping of palm butter and rice, his father called for "the weapon." The boy knew the ritual well. Slowly, he retrieved the eighteen-inch silver stew spoon, its red strap dangling like a warning. His mother's hands had once hung it carefully to dry. Now it was his shame.

Before the stern faces of government men, Boikai Senior struck his son for failing to build bonds with classmates in America. "Don't spoil this thing here," his father screamed. The boy fell, his rage swallowed, his humiliation complete. Disappointment overshadowed the room. His mother reached for her son, but he turned away from her. On the ivory and gold tiles lay the remnants of his heart's warmth, shaken, spilled, and forever lost.

But even in the shadow of their father's fury, the bond between the brothers held fast. Pain tightened its grip on the house, yet Boikai Junior's resolve only deepened, a silent vow forming in the cracks of his shame.

"I will always protect my brother," Boikai said after a quarrel with his father. Boima stayed with his parents at home, going to the market on the waterside with their house girl, Bertha, and returning to draw the market, its design, and the town's people from memory. He captured men selling packs of Presidential cigarettes, even the intricate details of the large umbrellas shielding the vendors and their goods.

Boikai told his father that he should put Boima's drawings in a museum. Their father, Boikai Senior, said, "Where should I send them first, the Louvre? Stop with this foolishness and do what I spent your school fees on. Don't worry about Boima; he's not at the capacity I need to further our mission."

The mission Boikai's senior had was just bullshit. What would come to pass with Liberia? No, pleading with schoolmates at Covington would not strengthen the country's relations. All his father knew was that his hope for Boikai in junior year was only self-serving and would fracture trust within his son.

The dance hall rocked that July 26th evening in 1978. Independence Day felt all too liberating for Boikai. During his internship at the Ministry of Agriculture, not long after graduating from Covington Episcopal School in 1972, he had taken his loneliness and homesickness and forged an alter ego with two faces: the quiet scholar who kept his head down and the jovial African boy who could outdrink the fattest boy in his class.

No one could keep up with him. Survival meant outsmarting and outdrinking those privileged white boys. No one peed on his uniform after he outdrank Alistar Wilcox.

Briarwood Academy, just over from Covington, was a place of manicured lawns and endless knolls—a finishing school for young debutantes and the most coveted on the Northeastern seaboard. Four former First Ladies had once walked its halls, and its name carried prestige, poise, and expectation.

Yet even within those hallowed walls, the thrill of rebellion called. Every so often, the Covington boys—Boikai among them—slipped across the grass to steal moments with the restless daughters of privilege. One in particular caught his eye: Fiona Barclay. Her family was wealthy, her status enviable, but her heart longed for the forbidden—an entanglement with the young African prince.

One stormy night, Boikai scaled the trellis to her dormitory window. Inside, Fiona's roommate, Donna Mayfield, lay beneath her covers, longing for sleep as whispers and muffled gasps filled the room. In the chaos, an equestrian trophy toppled, and Headmistress Agatha Macintosh burst through the door. Boikai darted into the closet, clutching only his underwear. Fiona, calm and unflinching, claimed a nightmare had startled her. The headmistress barked for quiet and left.

Boikai dressed quickly, pressed a parting kiss upon Fiona, and descended the trellis into the night, disappearing before dawn as though he had never been there at all.

He graduated at the top of his class. The administration couldn't believe his marks; they made him retake the tests, and he conquered them again. They had no choice but to make the African scholar their first Black valedictorian.

Like they say back home, "Hmmm, that's sweet for you." Boikai savored the stunned look on the headmaster's face. He gifted the school three boxes of his mother's Ivory Soap Flakes and left without looking back.

After the sixth song from the Fifth Dimension, the crowd strained their voices to "Up, Up and Away in My Beautiful Balloon!" Kebbeh Johnson entered. Her palm-butter skin would make any man go weak. She walked in wearing periwinkle bell-bottom pants, a blue top, a yellow head tie, her black, outstretched hair peeking out, and gold hoop earrings. Kebbeh could cuss out any man who looked at her sideways.

She was fierce, brash, and could outdrink any grown man, and no one would mess with her. At first, Boikai was intimidated. He was gobsmacked by her presence. He asked her to dance when Bunny Mack came on. "Come on, my sweetie, my sugar," he said.

Kebbeh swung her head and shouted, "My man, if you recite this song just to play with me, I will slap your mouth. You better move from here."

Boikai grabbed Kebbeh's waist. "Your hard head will get you no husband."

She laughed, put her drink down, and followed him to the dance floor. They slow-danced to Bunny Mack, their hips in perfect sync. They left the hall together that night and had a beautiful morning.

Before daybreak, while in bed in Boikai's apartment, she shared her hopes to open her own magazine company. She had big ambitions; Kebbeh had just graduated with a Journalism degree from Liberty University in the rural part of the country. She lived with her mother in a small apartment above Nabil's Mechanic Shop on Carey Street. Her vulnerability was as warm as the sheets on his bed.

This was the first time Boikai had ever felt truly seen—raw and unguarded with a woman. While he showered, Kebbeh joined him, and they made love one last time before he left to visit his obligatory companion.

With her shoes in hand, Boikai brushed her cheek and whispered, "We can only be together in private." Kebbeh already knew he was spoken for. Their love, however fierce, had to stay hidden.

"Everybody's business in the bush is our country's business," Kebbeh teased. "I am a journalist; let me be your pepperbird. You won't even see me, my love. I will fly away and go about my business. Our love will be correct in our eyes, not in what the people say outside."

Boikai cupped her face, wiped away her tears, and kissed her. He brushed her hair back and pinned it as if fastening armor for a woman the world refused to love. Then he dressed quickly, spraying extra cologne to mask the scent of their forbidden embrace. Shame settled over him like a shadow—the old fear of humiliation and the memory of his father's blows reminding him of the force he could never overcome.

But outside voices carried farther than love's whisper. Their parents had already arranged Boikai's marriage to Beatrice, sealing the match soon after her baptism. Kebbeh's bold, outspoken nature revealed the kind of partner Boikai truly wanted—a woman unafraid to lead, not the docile housewife he saw in Beatrice.

Is my own weapon a game for these women? Boikai wondered. *Must I wound the woman I love to appease the woman I am bound to?*

Kebbeh knew her family would never climb Liberia's upper echelon. She also carried dangerous knowledge about the Hintons—secrets that could not be spoken. Her pursuit of Liberia's promising young statesman was not a mere chance but a careful move toward her own future.

Yet tradition chose Beatrice, and with that choice the course of generations quietly shifted.

Chapter 4: Kebbeh

Every generation in a Liberian family was a girl born with the inheritance of being a force to be reckoned with. She walked the earth to the beat of her own drum, yet people were mesmerized by her entrance into a room. They wanted to learn her story when they locked eyes. They yearned to know how she came to be and how she could command any place she encountered. The most revered were envious of her innate power, yet she was a truth teller with the internal scars she carried. She knew too much.

"**A** hard head makes a soft ass!" Kebbeh's mother, Ma Eliza, had run out of patience with her for refusing to wear her schoolgirl uniform. Kebbeh was stubborn—even in the fourth grade. She preferred to wear pants, but that was not the requirement of her heavy cotton navy blue jumper dress and white cotton button-down shirt. St. Tabitha's Convent School was full of pride and status. Parents throughout the bustling city of Monrovia clambered their way to enroll their child in St. Tabitha's. If you were the lucky few enrolled in this all-girls academy, your daughter could write her own ticket to Liberia's elite class.

"Trousers are for loose girls. Why can't you just dress like a lady?" her mother shouted from their kitchen in their two-bedroom apartment above Nabil's Mechanic Shop.

Kebbeh stared out her window, counting the eyelet holes in her curtains. She calmed down when she reached her favorite number—99. Then she ironed her jumper, stretched out her white button-down shirt—still carrying the scent of the humid Monrovian air from the day before—and got dressed.

People used to say that she came into this world like a lioness; she was born during a horrible thunderstorm and had screamed her way ever since. She was the only child of her mother. Born in secret, she never met her father, but her mother always told her she would not want to know him.

The way Kebbeh's mother sold her oranges—how she wrapped them, how buyers bargained over their price—was a dance of quiet defiance. Each gesture carried rhythm, each word its own step in the marketplace ballet. Impatience flickered across her face when someone toyed too long with her livelihood, yet her voice never wavered.

Kebbeh saw it all: her mother's conversations with customers were more than simple exchanges. Each sale was a sacrifice, another stone laid toward her daughter's education, each coin a prayer answered. Some grumbled that the oranges cost too much, but Kebbeh understood. For her mother, every act of service at that stall was a whispered thanksgiving to God for what He had already done.

Ma Eliza often told the story herself. "He was a crooked man," she said, "who had no business with me but would always drive up to my orange stand."

Her father was said to wear a charcoal grey tweed suit and a Panama hat. He would purchase only one orange and flirt with Ma Eliza, promising her the world.

When her mother got with Mr. Tweed Suit, his promises turned violent. He did not know she was even pregnant. Once he found out that she had Kebbeh, her mother had to set up shop on Benson Street and wear a wig for two years. Deep down, Kebbeh carried an aching fear of running into Mr. Tweed Suit. Would he wait for her at the school gate and take her from her mother? She examined the faces of the men she encountered, always subtly searching for the crooked man who was her father, lurking in the shadows of her greatest fear. From the day she learned her mother's secret, she feared any man in town wearing a Panama hat.

Ma Eliza was so desperate to have a home for herself and her daughter that she decreased her rent by giving Nabil three bushels of oranges each week in exchange for the apartment. It cut deeply into her profits, but a roof over their heads was more important than extra money. They had no choice.

When Ma Eliza's father discovered she was with child, he threw her out of the house. Nabil's apartment became her refuge, a place where no one questioned a mother with a small girl by her side selling oranges after Sunday service.

From the time Kebbeh crouched beneath her mother's mahogany table, arranging paper dolls in the dust, she absorbed a truth that would anchor her life: she would never need a man to care for her. The scents of roasted peanuts, sliced mango, and fresh-cut oranges drifted through the market air as her mother's voice rose and fell like a drumbeat—steady, firm, sure.

"You can take care of yourself," her mother said, hands flashing as she tied bags, weighed produce, and exchanged cash. Kebbeh watched those hands with awe—strong enough to lift heavy buckets, gentle enough to peel an orange into perfect spirals.

She carried that strength proudly into the world beyond the market. At school, when classmates whispered about wealth and pedigrees, Kebbeh held her chin high. She boasted without hesitation: her mother was a big businesswoman at Dunbar General Market. No student dared challenge her. The very fact that Kebbeh walked the halls of such a prestigious school was proof enough—her mother's labor, sacrifice, and defiance woven into every confident step she took.

She knew if her mother could do it and make a name for herself, so could Kebbeh. They said Nabil, who hailed from

Lebanon, had escaped persecution in the late 1950s and found Liberia to be a welcoming place. Although he was in the minority, he always turned a blind eye when Kebbeh's mother allowed her and any female relative to stay with them for a month or two after their husbands returned to their real wives.

Kebbeh's Aunty Sarah carried a branding burn on her forearm—her husband's initials. He claimed that if she ever lay with another man, he would know. As a child, Kebbeh traced the raised letters, BW, on her aunt's arm to soothe herself at night—never knowing it was her tag of shame.

At St. Tabitha's, the halls gleamed marigold and navy blue, the school colors. The nuns marched in formation, shepherding pupils to classrooms lined with large ebony benches, roll-top desks, and two miniature green lights perched atop elongated mahogany tables in the parish library. Between Sister Mary Teresa's catechism lessons, the daughters of society buzzed with gossip.

Kebbeh buried herself in her studies, though echoes of laughter still haunted the halls. They had not forgotten the day Sister Mary Elizabeth discovered her petition—scrawled in bold letters across yellow paper—requesting trousers be added to the girls' uniforms. With a swift tear, the nun shredded it before Kebbeh could present it at morning assembly. The scraps fluttered to the floor like broken feathers, and with them, Kebbeh's small act of defiance became another joke among her classmates.

To Kebbeh, the pomp and circumstance of St. Tabitha's were nothing more than pageantry—a fragile performance mimicking what America possessed without holding its freedom. She saw it clearly: they were training her to revere the very masters of her oppression. The surnames whispered with reverence in those halls determined privilege, and she carried none of them.

Yet she carried something greater, her mother's vision. Every long night at the market, every coin exchanged across worn wooden tables was a sacrifice meant to place Kebbeh in these rooms of ultimate power. She understood her purpose. One day, she would not merely endure the weight of their rules. She would turn history itself on its head.

Although Kebbeh was not Catholic, her mother worked tirelessly at the orange stand to pay school fees. She could not risk her daughter's expulsion, nor could she stir trouble with the sisters. Weekly, Kebbeh stayed after school to scrub the nunnery floors. If the floor passed Sister Mary Elizabeth's tight inspection, Kebbeh could use the washing machine to clean her uniform. She loved mathematics and excelled in French, and each small triumph fueled her quiet rebellion.

Her schoolmate Marguerite, a heavy-set girl with soft, coily curls, was her comrade. Marguerite could cuss out any boy at St. Peter's Catholic School across the courtyard, and she and Kebbeh walked to and from school together. The girls got into plenty of trouble. In seventh grade, they freed the class rabbit. Sister Irene grabbed a switch from the mango tree and whipped them both. The rabbit didn't make it far. That evening, one of the old ma's up the roadside made rabbit stew.

Sister Irene cried as she whipped them. The sting could not match the ache in the rabbit's eyes, trapped and helpless. The girls had believed they were liberating it, unaware of its true fate.

"They prayed that Saint Peter might bring it back to life, like he had with Saint Tabitha," Marguerite whispered.

"Marguerite, you stupid girl, Saint Peter has bigger things to do," Kebbeh retorted. Their laughter lingered, tethering them forever to that fateful day in seventh grade.

One bustling Saturday at Dunbar Market, the air thickened with the scent of fried plantains, diesel fumes, and ripened fruit. Kebbeh crouched behind her stall, fingers busy tying bushels of oranges with twist ties, though her ears caught every word around her. Two men in pressed suits stood a few feet away, their voices sharp, edged with promise and anger.

"Liberia will finally get what is owed to us," one declared. The other nodded, jaw set like granite.

Kebbeh lowered her head slightly, concentrating, yet her eyes followed every detail—the cut of their jackets, the polish of their shoes, the weight they carried in their movements. Were they men of government, or merely shadows trailing those who ruled? She had to know.

With practiced grace, she handed them their bag of oranges, hands steady even as her heart raced. She watched them join a group of younger men at the edge of the market—boys with restless eyes, men with little to lose. Kebbeh felt it then, as if history itself had brushed past her stall: change was circling, gathering, waiting for its moment to strike.

Kebbeh's first job at the *Liberian Gazette* in 1980 was as the society relations reporter. Her position was to cover events involving the crème de la crème of Liberian society. From society balls at the Executive Mansion to weddings of justices' children, Kebbeh's byline carried the whispers of high society.

She had access to invitations, and the newspaper gave her a small budget to dress the part. The invitations arrived at The Gazette; after all, no one of true status lived above an auto body shop. She attended each event as press. One night, wearing a peach bell-sleeve chiffon gown, white pumps, and a bouffant hairstyle, she was determined to look like she belonged.

In her hand, she carried a miniature tape recorder and microphone. On her left hand rested a thin gold ring that turned her finger green, but appearances mattered. She needed society to believe she had a husband at university abroad. There was no husband. The ruse was her protection from high-powered men and their advances.

At one ball, while welcoming the King and Queen of Denmark, a senator made a pass at her. Kebbeh slapped him so hard his tooth loosened. Still, she blended back into the crowd, quietly taking notes. To the outside world, they carried on. But Kebbeh felt a duty to share with her countrymen what happened behind closed doors.

The elite whispered that she was a spy for the common man. Jeers and stares followed her across marble floors. She met their eyes with a gaze so unflinching it made wives clutch their husbands tighter. Recording the conversations of the wealthy gave her the details she needed for her stories.

But business was never the only reason she attended. Kebbeh often saw the love of her life with his woman of obligation. Boikai and Beatrice attended nearly every event they were assigned to.

Kebbeh, holding her tape recorder, interviewed the new Minister of Commerce—Boikai. Endorsed by Beatrice's father, he had been groomed for this role since college. The country was eager to see what he would accomplish.

Kebbeh held her head high, eyes on the women clutching desperately at their men. *You marry to share life with someone, not to depend on them for survival,* she thought.

As the couple entered, Beatrice and Kebbeh locked eyes. Their silent battle became routine, a contest of who would break the gaze first. Kebbeh never had time for Beatrice's foolishness, though a pang of ache lingered in her heart for the other woman.

Why would a woman stay with a man who never loved her? Kebbeh wondered. Was it self-loathing, or a determination to keep him no matter what?

She knew Beatrice would never give her compassion if their roles were reversed. And deep down, she feared Boikai's hunger for status meant he would never truly be hers.

Her womb swelled as Beatrice's did.

After one interview, Boikai slipped with Kebbeh into the butler's quarters of the Chief Justice's compound. In the cold, dark room, between the icebox and wine storage, he whispered: "When Beatrice has the baby, I'm leaving her. I can't continue this charade. I overheard her calling some friend in Paris named John."

"How will you possibly leave your wife and newborn?" Kebbeh challenged. "You'll be ostracized. We have too much to lose. I can't risk my job so you can abandon her."

Boikai wept against the icebox, and once again, they surrendered to passion. When it ended, they composed themselves, kissed one final time, and parted. Kebbeh straightened her gown, flushed and upset. She had surrendered to his charisma again—and that's what got her pregnant in his car that cold evening on the beach.

She surrendered her love for him so that he could continue the mask of love he had for Beatrice. I pray to Papa God that He will give me and my child in my womb His guidance and protection. I will go on to report that the tea and kala were piping hot, along with Justice Roberts discussing Afrofuturism, overlooking his newly built tennis court.

While Kebbeh dictated the grand march dance in the parlor, describing the men and women of Liberian society in their silk gowns, their hairstyles echoing European fashion, stepping two by two in a trance-like rhythm of order, pomp, and circumstance—she felt her baby kick for the first time. It shook her to the core. *My baby is kicking,* she thought, a thrill of surprise mixed with sudden sadness washing over her.

Beatrice believed safety and security were the only keys to surviving life with her new husband. She felt bound by duty, destined to play a role cloaked in servitude to a man more eager to free himself than to ever free his wife.

Kebbeh, in contrast, longed for something different. Her love for Boikai was fierce, but secrecy had turned it bitter. Each stolen glance, each hushed meeting, carried the weight of scandal. To the world, their bond was a whisper; to her heart, it was a prison sentence, tightening with every passing day, offering little hope of escape.

She couldn't tell his father about the kick—he was busy dancing with his bride. *Any hint of my joy would expose this sham of a marriage and the shame of our relationship. My sweet baby, growing inside me—your life is too sacred for this circle of snobs, feasting on delicacies served on imported china. You're destined to see through the farce of birthright status.*

Keep kicking, my strong baby. We'll be alright. Your mother was raised with no Pa—you'll be alright, oh. I'll be both a good mother and a good father to you, She declared.

They left Justice Roberts' party early. Kebbeh wasn't sure if her nausea came from the cigar smoke lingering near security or the smug, victorious look Beatrice cast from across the hall.

Chapter 5: James

The prodigal son with no father is the illusion of manhood. How shall I walk this earth without guidance but sheer abandonment? The feeling of not knowing who you are and yearning for the glance of your older self looking back at you. The mirrors of your truth are mired by the suffering of your mother. Will she share, or will you forgive her forced separation of your divine connection?

James Siaka Johnson was of the second generation to be born a secret. Boikai visited his mother, Kebbeh's, apartment so infrequently that his visits were more of an inconvenience for this young child. The surprising fact was that James never met his father, or at least that was what he was to know.

The infrequent visitor expected young James to address him as Uncle Kai. It was customary in Liberian culture to address adults in one's life with the "Uncle" and "Aunty" precursor to one's name, but for young James, it only led to more confusion. Why did this tall black man want me to call him 'Uncle'? My mother never had siblings, and the way they treat each other, why would I call her boyfriend Uncle?

Boikai kept the respect for James at arm's length. He often ignored James and never nurtured him, and barely hugged the child. While James watched this uncle come and go in his mother's bedroom, James would take his little sister outside to play when his mother entertained Uncle Kai.

When James was seven, a car backfired downstairs, startling him so badly that he grabbed a butter knife and tried to open his mother's locked door. His ingenuity pushed it ajar, and the scream that tore from his throat when he saw his mother entangled with Uncle Kai made him grab his sister. They hid beneath the awning of the nearby speaker store until the rain washed over them.

From that day on, every time Uncle Kai returned, James avoided eye contact and took his sister by the hand without explanation, allowing his mother and her boyfriend uninterrupted privacy. He carried a quiet sense of being an inconvenience, a cold understanding that he and his sister had to fend for themselves. Fingers gripping hers tightly to keep her from running into the street or disappearing into the crowd, James learned to navigate danger alone. The ache lingered, and the scent of hot sweat mixed with shoe polish transported him back to those early lessons in vigilance—back to the moment the butter knife clattered to the floor.

While James softly kicked his football between his feet, he overheard his grandmother and his mother, Kebbeh, arguing at the kitchen table. "What if his wife finds you with him in your place, Kebbeh? These people are too powerful. They will spoil your reputation, oh."

Kebbeh snapped, "What power, Ma? These people are now at our level. What was the old guard of society has consequently been burned down. Beatrice is a common woman like me now; she is trying to survive, too. She has no time to come looking for her husband, and he knows that.

"Besides, she's in the States with her daughter; she will never come back here." James stood motionless; the thought of this man's wife scared him. Could Uncle Kai's wife kill him and his sister? Or his mother, or even worse, his grandmother? The shiver down his spine awakened him out of his stillness. He turned to his sister, playing with her smart Sally doll, and made an excuse to go play outside. He would lie awake at night envisioning the day a woman would come looking for his family and seeking revenge because of his mother's choice to lie in bed with a married man.

Boikai had another family in America. He would leave every July to visit Kebbeh and her children. Most days, James watched as he ate dry rice and drank orange juice and dry gin at their kitchen table. In between spoonfuls of rice and chewing on a chicken bone, he studied James up and down.

As James' feet dangled from the chair, he looked at him and said, "Doggit, this boy is a footballer, oh. Look at how he swings his foot—that's a power striker right there, oh, Kebbeh."

Kebbeh rolled her eyes. "No time for that football business. This boy will be a diplomat. His curiosity—and the way he solves other people's problems—are on point."

James felt that his so-called diplomatic skills weren't about statesmanship at all. They were surviving, a constant effort to keep the peace at home, to avoid being a problem for his mother as she navigated her entanglements with the man across the kitchen table. He was at war within himself, always seeking an exit from the very people God had assigned to care for him.

Watching his mother frown at his play-uncle's predictions, James studied Boikai's face, wondering if the man's prophecy held true. He loved watching Manchester United on television and imagined himself on the pitch, yet he couldn't shake the feeling that this man might be giving him false hope.

The tension between his parents made James wish Uncle Kai were there every day. Maybe then his family could return to Liberia. Meanwhile, his little sister Ruby rolled her plastic duck—with rubber wheels for legs—across the floor. Boikai paused and said quietly, "She looks like my daughter, Joviah."

Kebbeh snickered, snapping back, "Please, Boikai, don't say that name in my house. I don't want to hear that foolishness. Ruby is my child, and she looks like herself.

"Next thing you know, Boikai, you will say James looks just like you, and I would tell you that James looks like himself."

Boikai didn't argue with her. He looked straight at James, locked eyes, and said, "Hmmm, I beg you, Kebbeh, the lie you keep telling. That boy must be the son of the most handsome man in all of Liberia—James Brown. Didn't you interview him when he performed here? No wonder you gave that boy his Pa's name." James dreamed of having a father who loved him and wished this banter would be out of love and not scrutiny. He was never comfortable when this man would come around. He felt more at home when Uncle Kai was not around. This internal battle with what it meant to have an unconditional, loving home would ultimately cost him.

His laughter bellowed so loudly that he woke Gran-Gran on the sofa.

The song blaring Bunny Mack's "My Sweety, My Sugar" saturated the apartment, and it brought Kebbeh Johnson back to the fast times of her and Boikai's secret affair. The not-so-secret joy rides in Boikai's bright blue Monte Carlo down to Bayfront Beach. Kebbeh boasted to James that people would stop and whisper to each other because they were envious of me (and she pointed both thumbs at herself), with her chest puffed up with pride because of her status as a reporter, which went up tenfold because she was in Boikai Collins' car around town.

Feeling the pulse of the song that was their declaration of their unending love, Kebbeh knew that she loved Boikai and that their affair couldn't disrupt his job and family life in the United States. The shame continued to build as Kebbeh raised her children alongside her mother, who knew too well what it meant to raise a child with a negligent father.

The feeling of emptiness never solidified for James. He would forever wonder why he never acknowledged him as his son. Would the truth be too real for him to speak it into existence? Or did he want James to stay a secret so that his other family wouldn't be torn apart?

January 18, 1980 – The tensions in Monrovia drew closer. Under the hood of a crimson Fiat 8v, a stout Lebanese man emerged, grease seeping into his fingernails and sweat dripping down his thick cotton shirt: Nabil Hassan. He owned the Auto Shop below Kebbeh and Ma Eliza's apartment. He was a quiet man who did what he could to support his only daughter, Rabia—working legally in his business, and illegally when it was the only way to feed her.

The forty-five-year-old man was a hustler both in the shop and on the streets of Monrovia. He dealt drugs on the street and at The Coconut Husk Dance Hall. He was feared by most, and those who didn't fear him loathed him with incessant gossip and sabotage of his tools. His sensitive olive skin couldn't stand the heat of the black tar sizzle emanating from the pavement. His second prized possession was a thick gold chain around his neck that read "Too Rich" in cursive. This rugged landlord suggested to Kebbeh during her pregnancy to eat more hummus to give the baby "good skin."

Kebbeh laughed and cussed Nabil's name under her breath.

April 12, 1980 – The day the Lone Star fell. The rebels came in April and executed plenty of people in the old Talbot Administration. Killing the President, his cabinet members, and anyone associated with the head of state. The country was in complete chaos. The world watched in silence, and the allied forces watched in the comfort of their own homes, punishing this African republic for not complying with their expectations. It was a type of punishment on the backs of the Liberian people.

Everyone was a victim, and everyone was in danger. The ultimate governmental collapse led to a worldwide flogging with the superpowers at the helm. Kebbeh was extra careful reporting the news out of fear that the new President Dolay would jail her or execute her. He didn't care that she was pregnant. Dolay was killing many journalists who disagreed with his rule.

Three fateful months later, while Kebbeh went into labor with James at Kingsford Hospital, a terrible thunderstorm raged outside. She said "Uncle Kai" held her hand—but she squeezed it so hard, she nearly broke it. Every birthday, she told her son James how every rumble of thunder matched the intensity of her labor pains. Each time, she cried out, "Oh, James Siaka, please take it easy on me, oh."

James was given the middle name Siaka by the Vai people, which means "One who is firstborn." When James came to this world, Uncle Kai saw the child enter the world the way God designed it and passed out. Kebbeh said before Boikai hit the ground, he named him James Siaka Johnson.

He said to Kebbeh, "My son will be a diplomat one day, and diplomats need a name that sounds democratic."

Since that day, Kebbeh and Ma Eliza brought baby James home to that apartment above the auto shop. Every now and then, James watched his mother stare off into the distance, her eyes filled with sudden sadness. He tried his best to appease his mother and create a distraction by playing Bunny Mack for her on their record player. Kebbeh would awaken from her feelings of shame and regret and dance with her children. She had to pretend that everything was alright for her children. She picked up each child and spun them around. Their voices of laughter drowned out the constant noise of a mechanic's drill.

She bent down to James and locked eyes with her son, touched his small nose, and said, "You know that's our song. I love you forever, my future diplomat."

Ma Eliza, also known as Gran-gran to her grandchildren, was the enforcer of a peaceful home for her daughter and her children. She was small in stature, but had a booming voice of ten men. Although she was short, she looked up to her grandson. James knew if he gave her a hard time, he would feel a tongue lashing and a lashing on his behind before he could apologize. Her quiet voice commanded every room. She disciplined with grace and sternness. She loved her business. His favorite moments with

Gran-gran were when she bathed James when he was four years old. She would sing old hymns while she bathed him. She would rub lotion all over his face so fast and so hard that it would almost fall off. The way she would grease his scalp and his face with dona grease (shea butter to you non-Liberians reading). James looked forward to his time with Gran-gran because he felt he was born anew.

His skin shone in the night. Gran-gran had the reading level of a sixth grader, but the stories she told about her days in the market and who she saw were sagas in themselves. James loved his time with Gran-gran; she was his beacon of hope and the support that he never had besides his mother. He could tell her secrets, and she would put coconut candy in his pocket and wink at him. She would get up before dawn. Tie her lappa across her waist, recite her devotionals, sip some warm Ovaltine, and take her small pink pocketbook and wares to the market on Benson Street. There, she enjoyed gossiping with her friends, laughing. Making her cups out of oranges for any of her customers. She and her friends were the eyes and ears of Monrovia. They would see houseboys and housegirls purchasing goods and products for their bosses and their families. They would hear whispers and murmurs: who's getting married, who's going where, politics.

Before the government crumbled, Ma Eliza listened softly to all the voices at her stand in between scoring each of her oranges and asking for information. She was a trusted and respected vendor at the market. The servants, chauffeurs, houseboys, and housegirls would stop at her stand and purchase her oranges in exchange for news about what was happening in their homes of employment. Ma Eliza was determined. Every day, she set up her stand and listened to the murmurs and gossip, and brought it to her daughter. She closed up shop early to make sure she was home for James and Ruby when they got home from school. She set up their favorite snack, graham crackers with peanut butter and fresh-squeezed orange juice. She used only the leftover oranges that didn't sell that day at the market. James loved that woman with his whole heart. She was his second mother and confidante.

She always said, "Nothing is wrong with you, and don't let anybody tell you otherwise." He felt safest in her arms.

The fighting intensified. Rebels advanced on the capital of Monrovia on Christmas Eve, 1991. Child soldiers and rebel leaders stormed the city. The whizzing of gunshots cut through the air. The Lone Star was about to sink into another depth of despair, the kind born of its own making. Eleven-year-old James spent long days curled in a ball, crawling on his stomach to the bathroom. Curfew didn't exist. Mortar fire made sleep impossible.

The day of Christ's birth was marked by fear rather than celebration. That morning, Kebbeh, her mother, James, and Ruby walked to the French Embassy. Kebbeh knew the French ambassador from her years at the newspaper. He promised to get her and her children out of Liberia. They left with tears in their eyes, abandoning their beloved mother and grandmother. Ma Eliza, a stubborn patriot, feared nothing God intended for her life. She knelt before James and said, "I was born in Liberia, I will die in Liberia."

She kissed her daughter and grandchildren, and the family slipped out under the cover of night, hearts racing faster than the gunfire whizzing through the air. Holding only fear and the strength to keep running, they made their escape. The French government granted them asylum, and they flew out of Liberia the next morning—Kebbeh had shared government information with them, a dangerous act that could have cost her life the moment she touched down in Monrovia.

When the family landed on French soil, James screamed for his grandmother. The sound tore through the cabin, raw and desperate, because deep down he knew he would never see her again. A French flight attendant knelt beside him, pressing two shiny airplane pins into his hand as if a trinket could seal his breaking heart. But the pins felt cold, meaningless against the searing truth: he was leaving a piece of himself behind.

How could he call this freedom when the woman who raised him had chosen to meet death in the soil of her people? His grandmother's choice became a wound that would not heal—a reminder that home was not just a place but a presence, a heartbeat he could no longer reach.

His mother, worn down by her own storms of choice, offered no embrace, no words to comfort his grief. He had learned early that sorrow had to be swallowed in silence. So when they stepped out of Charles de Gaulle airport, he buried his longing for home and the memory of his grandmother deep in the hidden chambers of his soul.

And yet, in that act of burial, something stirred: an instinct to endure. If home could no longer be a country or a grandmother's lap, perhaps it could be found in the fragile safety of his family's survival. He would carry his grief like a trunk—tucked away but never forgotten—and let it shape him into someone capable of rebuilding in exile.

The Johnsons settled in a small apartment on Rue Camou near the Arc de Triomphe. As a high schooler, James found solace at football practice with his friends after classes. Their school was a train ride away in Paris. Other Liberian expats populated the city, a community that became the closest thing to home. They depended on one another to succeed in a foreign land, recreating laughter, warmth, and the familiarity of family for their children within the walls of St. Vincent's, in the heart of Paris.

His schoolmates, Thomas and Geoffroy, were the children of ambassadors from Nigeria and Côte d'Ivoire. The boys would go through the metro on Saturdays and sneak into Paris Saint-Germain football games. They were finally caught by security, which led them to work at the stadiums to get a glimpse of their favorite football players.

The one girl that James felt was the one who got away was Rabia, Nabil's daughter from back home. Nabil used all the money he had to send Rabia to Paris to live with her aunt Rasha. Nabil was very stubborn and did not want to leave Liberia, so he sent his only daughter to meet an aunt she barely knew by herself. Rabia was his first and true love. She was the statuesque, 5-foot-8 beauty with hazelnut skin, looking like a combination of an

African queen and a Mediterranean goddess. Her mother had been a beautiful Bassa woman.

Nabil loved her mother with all his heart. Unfortunately, she died during childbirth with Rabia. Nabil used all that he had to keep his daughter safe. And told stories of her mother every chance he got when he was with Rabia.

Her aunt did a good job, though, and raised Rabia in Paris. Rabia loved the city. She always told James that she wanted her own atelier overlooking the Seine when she grew up. She was an artist. She loved to paint, but she wasn't quite confident in herself. She always sought reassurance in everything she did. James always picked her up at the intersection of Rue Camou and Rouge, near Walker, and then they took the metro to class every morning.

They spoke in French and a little Liberian English, careful that other passengers wouldn't overhear. Both carried big, impossible dreams. James wanted to be a power striker for Paris Saint-Germain, while Rabia imagined her own art gallery in the heart of the city.

She missed Liberia. She missed her father, who had been tragically killed during the war while trying to save his neighbors and his business. The auto mechanic shop had taken a mortar hit in the middle of the night. He had tried to help his tenants in Kebbeh's old apartment escape, but it was too late—they all perished. Rabia vowed never to return to Liberia, bitter over how her father had been treated. She had always felt Nabil was more Liberian than Lebanese and that his people had betrayed him.

James understood her grief. He understood the sacrifice her father had made so she could live, so she wouldn't witness what he endured. The darkness that had overtaken Liberia weighed heavily on him. He wanted Rabia to remember the goodness of their country before it was consumed by war.

On their last day of twelfth grade, James invited Rabia to their little apartment. Kebbeh and Ruby were at a school play. James tried to cook her favorite fufu and okra gravy, hoping his quirky humor might lift her spirits.

"Umm, James, this fufu is lumpy, and did you cook frozen okra?"

Rabia laughed so hard, she nearly choked. James shook his head in embarrassment with a laugh, "Look, my Gran-gran didn't have a microwave back home to teach me, I tried oh."

Rabia smirked at a glance and said, "You're a better footballer than a cook, chey, it's rough." Rabia kept laughing until she was sweating. James knew his lack of culinary skills put a smile on his beloved's face. Rabia fulfills his sense of presence. She understood him more than he knew himself. She would let him crumple in pain when a memory arrived inside him of his beloved grandmother. She let him feel the hurt without the ridicule that he would receive from his mother's voice. She was his home, his peace, his sense of being alive without secrecy. They felt free without fear of betraying anyone.

They moved their laughter to the couch and spent most of the evening holding hands and kissing while *Living Single* blared on the television with the French translation dubbed in the background. Their bodies intertwined, and passion ensued. The movement was untamed, clinging to what they had fantasized about, which was so precious and real. She knew his secrets, and he knew the curves of her body. Their sweat dampened the couch cushions, and their whispers were drowned out by the laugh track on television, not realizing they had pushed the volume too high. They didn't notice Kebbeh and Ruby coming home early.

The shock of Kebbeh catching her son with his girlfriend was a surprise in reverse to the butter knife incident so many years ago.

"What's this?!" shouted Kebbeh.

James and Rabia, with her bra in hand, leapt from the couch.

Rabia, flushed with shame, said, "I'm sorry, ma," and ran out of the apartment.

James turned and watched Ruby cling to her mother in fear, and said to his mother, "Ruby isn't watching me as an example; she's watching you. A woman who won't let her children know their own father, or is that what a fast woman would do?"

Chapter 6: Foday

"Worry me, or give me a chance?" Foday whispered, desperate to be heard. A man chasing redemption without hope would perish in a pit of his own despair. He carried himself like the black mamba— silent, dangerous, ready to strike at anyone who questioned his worth.

Foday Freeman always carried a hidden fire, a score he could never settle. He moved in silence, but his eyes churned with the darkness that had long clouded the Freeman household. The irony of his last name was bitter. Foday had never felt free under the shadow of his father, the Baptist minister. His father preached redemption and forgiveness from the pulpit, but at home, he made Foday the sacrificial lamb—an example of what it meant to stray from God.

At the dinner table, scripture became a weapon. Verse after verse was thrown like a test of Foday's devotion, and if he stumbled, he paid in hunger. Supper was withheld as punishment. More nights than he could count, he cried himself to sleep, only to feel his mother's quiet hand slip a plate beneath his bed.

"Don't tell your father," she whispered, her voice trembling with both love and fear.

The clinking of hidden dishes beneath him became the secret soundtrack of his boyhood—proof that she could not disobey her husband openly, but also that she would never let her son starve. By day, Foday learned other lessons: toughness meant survival. At J.R. Clements School, he fought nearly every boy on the playfield. His husky stature gave him an advantage, but it was the hot, relentless rage that made him dangerous. Each fist he threw was meant for his father, though it landed on classmates who dared to laugh or cross him. On the surface, he was a brute, feared and unyielding. But inside, he was a boy suffocating under scrutiny, a minister's son who could never be good enough, never redeemed in the eyes that mattered most.

He told himself that if no one would protect him, he would carve out his own armor. Yet in the stillness after each fight, when the adrenaline subsided, what lingered was not victory but the ache of being unseen. Foday's pride made him defiant, but his fear that redemption would always remain just out of reach hardened him into someone no authority or savior could subdue.

"Foday! If I catch your ass back at that dance hall, there will be hell to pay." Minister Freeman's voice thundered from the pulpit of Redeemer Baptist Church in Caldwell.

The Reverend's white handkerchief, stitched with blue letters reading *Jesus is Lord*, dabbed at his dripping face. Foday's hands clenched, ready for the battle he had been urging all his life. Was this the moment he had been waiting for? The church ushers organized their Bibles and offering envelopes between the pews, then dropped the envelopes and scurried to the fellowship hall so the father could chastise his son in private.

Someone in the congregation must have reported seeing Foday drinking beer at the dance hall. He felt stalked by their eyes, as if the entire church had deputized itself to monitor his every move.

Foday hated the surveillance. He was grown, working, contributing to the household, and yet he was still treated like an errant child. Storming out of their third-floor apartment above the All Seasons Electronic Shop on Alton Street, he muttered, "My father will not determine the steps God has for me."

If God is merciful, why can't my father be? That moment—feeling the spray of saliva on his face—threw him back to the nights he ate cold fried plantain and dried fish gravy under his bed. All he could do was endure his father's verbal lashings. He couldn't defeat the congregation's most revered minister in the house of the Lord. Though rage roared through him, Foday knew that any argument he offered would be met with six Bible verses his father would recite to crush the debate.

When Foday drifted, wiping the spit from his face, he turned to his father and said, "You may have a big mouth and power here, but at home, your own wife defies you."

Foday left the pulpit behind, carrying the quiet vindication won at the price of his mother's compassion.

Unlike his friends, Foday had never gone to college. His passion was cars. At Nabil's shop, he learned the rhythm of engines, the thrill of repairs. On lucky days, a luxury car would roll in, and he and Nabil would take it for a spin through Monrovia before calling the owner. Zipping past taxis and motorbikes, Foday felt alive—as if he were a race car driver, a man of importance, the kind who turned heads and drew women effortlessly. He especially enjoyed joyrides with the fast girls from East Parochial Academy. They loved the thrill, and Foday felt the control of the cars was his and his alone. His customers knew he skimmed off Nabil's profits, charging extra under the cunning pretense of polishing and detailing that couldn't be found anywhere else.

The air in the shop shifted whenever she was near. His chest puffed before his eyes even found her. Steam from the bowls of jollof rice curled upward, carrying the sound of Kebbeh's voice.

Her bright smile lit up the shop. The men stopped, looking up at the girl, who bridged them with her favorite dish, thanking Nabil for allowing her family to live upstairs when the market was slow that summer of 1979. She wore a bright green dress with orange tiger-print stripes, an orange lily affixed to her braids. A month earlier, he had met Kebbeh helping at her mother's stand. The way she held his hand a little longer while he paid her made him feel she wanted to go on a future ride with him.

Foday was mesmerized by her smile. He suddenly realized he had dropped his drill on the ground. Her roaring laughter made him want to hide under the car he was working on.

"Nabil, my mother made you some jollof rice to thank you for your patience," she said.

Nabil said, "That's okay, the more she keeps feeding me like this, she won't have to pay for a year. I can barely buckle my trousers."

She glanced over at Foday and said, "There's plenty of rice for you here, just make sure you don't drop your bowl in the engine."

Foday smirked and said, "Fine girl like you, made me drop all my senses. How about I take you out, and I promise I won't drop you."

Kebbeh liked his quick wit and his capability to laugh at himself. She entertained the fact that he was a handsome man with an intriguing scar on his forearm. Her gentle touch allowed

Foday to let her in. She never threatened him or made him feel unworthy of love. She saw past his granite-like exterior and let his vulnerability wash through. No one else listened to him or his aspirations of moving out of his parents' apartment and opening his own shop.

Kebbeh held his hand, stroked his hair, and just listened. The way she looked in his eyes, he felt that he could inspire the plan he had seen Kebbeh serving him rice at her own shop, wearing trousers that were too big, and a baby growing in her belly. Like sand, spilling through his fingers is as fast as time will slip away from this vision of love he so longed for.

That evening, they ate at Yatta's Fish House and strolled along the beach before sunrise. They made love until the fisherman arrived, and he walked her home. Foday knew Kebbeh was the one for him. Little did he know, Kebbeh was already entangled with another man he would soon meet.

Foday heaved buckets of oranges at Ma Eliza's stand, sweat soaking his shirt. Boikai stopped by, his chauffeur walking ten feet behind him, asserting his presence. Boikai, flashing his signature smile, ignored the man restocking the oranges for the businesswoman. He spoke to Kebbeh in a voice that could make a church elder clutch her pearls. Kebbeh laughed at the man, unafraid to show exactly how he wanted her attention. As he paid her, the glint of his gold wedding band caught the sun, and Kebbeh's fingers lingered in his hand long enough for Foday to notice.

A sharp pang struck his chest. Would God hear his cry, or would this man's allure steal away the one love that made him feel valued?

Six months later, Boikai returned to the shop. His muffler had come loose after hitting a rock on the roadside. Pulling up to the curb, he stepped out and dropped his keys at Foday's feet.

Boikai looked down at him and said, "Pekin, you can't snatch big man's keys?"

Foday grimaced. He wasn't a child; he was a grown man. Who was this man to address him as if he didn't matter?

With a toothpick between his teeth and a chuckle as loud as his muffler, Boikai spoke to Nabil about the problem. Nabil nodded, promising the repair would be completed by the end of the week. Foday stood silently, watching this man in his European pinstripe suit parade through the shop, boasting about his new pregnant wife, while Foday fantasized about taking that toothpick out of Boikai's arrogant mouth and shoving it in a place only the good Lord Himself would find.

As Boikai left, he motioned to Foday to come close. Foday leaned in and he said, "I better not catch a drop of grease inside my car, or you will feel it, my pekin." Boikai turned on his heels and went upstairs to Kebbeh's apartment, and pointed down to Foday and finished with, "I'm damn serious."

Foday had more power than he believed he had. He knew which clients at the shop would kill for any information on how this smug man spent government time philandering with a mistress. It could take a simple conversation with a governmental official, getting a tune-up, that could implode this man's reputation and livelihood. The rumor mill around town claimed that Boikai secured a high-level position in government due to his education. On the contrary, his father pissed off the big people in government, so he sacrificed his son to take the position because he was a been-to.

The day before Boikai was to pick up his prized possession, Foday picked up his girl, Kebbeh, to the beach. "I can't stand that small-toto man."

Of course, he didn't know the size of his toto, but it kept Foday ready to fight the man; he couldn't stand loving his girlfriend. Why did he have to compete for Kebbeh's devotion?

Kebbeh told Foday that she was in love with Boikai and said that she didn't want to keep playing with Foday.

Foday's heartbreak felt like the vision of his future with Kebbeh was shattered like glass of what was not yet to be. His reality of what would never be hit him like he was being punished for something he wanted more than anything in this world. "I don't want anything to jump inside of me, Foday. You won't have the money to take care of me and your baby." Kebbeh's refusal to go any further crushed Foday's dream of having a family with her and the dream mechanic shop he'd always wanted.

"What does Boikai have that I don't?" said Foday.

Kebbeh yelled, "Status! No one wants a mechanic's baby. See, you got grease all on the man's backseat. He will crucify you himself if he finds that on his seat." Foday wasn't afraid of Boikai and his status. If he could survive the wrath of his father through humiliation and shame, he didn't care about Kebbeh's lover.

Foday laughed and wiped the grease with his blue shirt. Foday was confused and said, "Besides, what status will he have? That man is married!

"What status do you have, Kebbeh? That man doesn't love you like I do. He's just using you; he will never leave his wife."

Shaken about hearing about her lover's wife, Beatrice, Kebbeh wrestled to the front seat and put her earrings back on.

While Foday followed her to the driver's seat, he said, "Beatrice and her people are too powerful. Boikai is only looking out for himself. At the very least, I would look out for you and our future children. I'm working my hardest at the auto shop to make a life for us."

The tension between the new former lovers was as thick as the red dust on Yancy Road.

"Hmm, Foday, what does Nabil have for you? He will never give you his business. I know from the gossip at my mom's stand that Nabil purposefully makes more problems for cars to keep breaking down so people keep bringing their cars to Nabil to fix."

The quarreling between them rumbled on over the beats of Parliament on the car radio—"When you're hot, you're hot, look at what you got." Trying his best to crawl back into his hardened persona, he vowed never to let a woman break him to the possibility of being loved. Foday tried his hardest to change the subject.

"See, I said even Parliament said you're too much." Kebbeh looked at him and started laughing.

Foday convincingly gave her a kiss and said, "Boikai is only looking out for himself. The big people in government are using him as a pawn. I know myself, and I'm looking out for you. My precious love, let me take care of you and our future, please, I beg you, mehn."

With the air sucking out of her teeth, Kebbeh got out of the car and walked the beach rocks home.

Kebbeh went back to Boikai.

Foday heard she got pregnant shortly after she got back. In Foday's heart, that child is the child he wishes they had together. In the sweat of fixing cars and hearing the small feet running above the shop years later, Foday would imagine James' face looking back at him. *He's the child I want, but he's not mine.* He felt the shouts of his father, reminding him of how unworthy he is to be a father to a child like James.

Ma Eliza set the glass of water on the table, her eyes sharp with judgment. "Kebbeh cries herself to sleep because of you," she muttered. "I wish she had never loved you."

The words broke through Foday, reopening a wound he thought had closed. Ma Eliza turned away, climbing the stairs with slow, heavy steps. She carried more than a glass—she carried the weight of her daughter's choices, her own regrets, and the spirit of a marriage that had taught Kebbeh what not to expect from men. The old lessons of beatings for cold soup, of questions silenced with fists, still haunted her bones.

Now, the orange stand was her salvation. Behind its baskets of fruit, she found both freedom and secrets—whispers of soldiers, rumors of revolt, news that this land might soon turn on itself. She could do nothing to stop it.

Chapter 7 Ma Eliza

The beating of the Sassa guided the dancers' movements. The hard shell of the gourd collided with the intricate beading as though it were a constellation of sound. The woman tugged at the cords and shook the gourd simultaneously, competing with the drums. The more the rhythms shook and the dancers pounded their feet into the soil, the sound never ceased. The beading began to crack and split the gourd. Who would guide them now?

Dunbar General Market came alive before the sun could climb the vista. Along the dusty streets, women and men spread their wares—bowls of rice, ground peas, and peppers—while Bill White's radio crackled with news from Monrovia. The chatter of customers tangled with the hum of political unrest. For many, the market was more than just trade; it was a means of survival and independence for those denied access to education or a stable living.

Ma Eliza moved through it all with her second sight. Trouble announced itself to her long before it arrived, and she leaned on that gift as both shield and weapon.

Speaking with Ma Coto at her sugar cane stand, she said, her voice steady, "I learned early. As a girl in Maryland County, I helped Papa on his rice farm and sold bitterball by the roadside to pay for school fees. No one could cheat me. If I sensed your spirit was kind, I gave you grace. If it was dark, I made sure you paid double. My gran gran always said, 'This one can see trouble before it comes, oh.' And she was right."

Ma Coto asked her, "You see me, how so?"

Ma Eliza looked at her friend and replied, "Your spirit is plenty sweet, oh."

Ma Coto said, "I beg you, mehn."

The two women laughed together. Yet her sight had cost her, too. She had once warned her mother not to climb into the German mission man's truck.

"Take Old Pa Carter's truck," she had begged.

But her mother chose the easier path for hauling the rice. The truck slipped at the river bend, and Eliza's prophecy came true.

She never forgot the flash of orange lappa and green shirt floating downstream. Her scream still echoed in her chest. That moment seared itself into her very bones.

From that day forward, she vowed never again to turn away from the breath of danger. Shadows became spiritual messengers. A sudden rustle, a shift of air, the smallest tremor—each was a dialect only she could decipher. What once froze her in fear now forged a tempered sheath of iron within her, a resolve to stand guard for herself and for all who could not raise a shield of their own.

At the age of seventeen, she moved to Monrovia. The Dunbar General Market on Benson Street was busy and plentiful. Motor oil clung to the air, mingling with the noise of laughter, koloqua, and car horns blaring. House boys and house girls carried wash bins atop their heads, filled with the market's fresh produce for their house owners. Everything arranged on the tabletops and plastic tarps was simple yet inviting. Hours of standing in the blatant heat or sudden downpours were not for the weak-willed. You needed a sharp tongue and quick negotiation skills to survive.

The scent of aftershave and palm butter brought her back to the pain of the man her second sight could not catch. His name was Charles Carrowell, and he worked in government. A lanky, tall, light-skinned man in a tweed suit, about thirty, he stopped by Eliza's stand like clockwork every Wednesday morning. His ugly straw hat, with black velvet trim, sat crookedly on his head. He smiled with a crooked grin, a toothpick pressed between his teeth.

He would step up to the shy, young girl's stand and say, "Hey, fine girl, how much to buy your oranges? Oh, you cut it too sweet for me to not buy nothing here."

Eliza knew from his piercing eyes and devilish grin that playing with him would lead to plenty of trouble. The evil she usually sensed hovered like a hushed spirit, but it did not come for him. She had never had that kind of attention from a man before, and there was something about his green eyes that entranced her. She had never seen a Black man with green eyes. He claimed his Pa was Portuguese. In hindsight, she knew it had been a lie.

Charles lingered at her stand, sweat dripping down his pink eyelet shirt and black leather shoes. Ma Satta from Paynesville, who sold onions at the neighboring stand, warned her, "That Carrowell man got a big mouth and trouble. Do not leave with that man, stay at your stand and mind your business."

"His wife, Mrs. Carrowell, beat his last girlfriend so badly that she couldn't hear in her right ear," Ma Satta added.

Eliza ignored the warning when Charles offered her a place to sleep. She had been staying at Redeemer Baptist Church, where Minister Freeman promised her free lodging if she cleaned the commodes and parish hall. But the Minister had taken advantage of her innocence after the secretary left. One night was all it took for her to run away from the church and sleep under her stand.

Bruised and trembling, she understood at last that survival was not merely the art of evading danger, but the skill of outplaying it. Her second sight wasn't as strong as she once believed, but her spirit refused to falter. From now on, every choice, every trust offered by a man, would pass through the blade's edge of her hard-won wisdom. What she had thought was iron in her bones was, in truth, the thickness of a calabash. She vowed to sharpen it, so that neither fate nor any hand claiming power over her would ever again dictate the path of her life—or the life of her child.

She left her mother's Bible in that parish hall. So when Mr. Carrowell returned that third Wednesday and promised her an apartment overlooking Nahweh Point, she had no choice but to let him stay with her.

The dark veil of her gift had failed her. Soon, she was pregnant and uncertain of who the father was—Mr. Carrowell or Minister Freeman. When she confessed her confusion to Carrowell, he beat her nearly to death. Yet Ma Eliza, broken in spirit and body, clung to the relief that baby Kebbeh remained safe in her womb.

Pregnant and scared, she resolved to make a life for herself and her child. Six months later, a man named Jahn Johnson took pity on her. Each night, after closing the bank where he worked, he saw her crawl under her stand to sleep. One morning, he gave her fifty dollars, saying, "For that baby in your stomach."

Their friendship turned into companionship, then into love. For the first time in Ma Eliza's life, she felt safe and began to dream of a family again. Mr. Johnson worked as a bank teller at the Liberian National Bank. His modest home and yellow Fiat 500 gave him the nickname Mr. Taxi.

They held a quiet beach ceremony with Kebbeh tied to her back. Life for this family of three was gentle and secure. Ma Eliza's joy grew as she carried Kebbeh on her back while building her orange vendor business.

But storms returned. One day, after a long climb home in the rain, her second sight failed her again. She found her husband in bed with the bank manager, Mr. Abraham. Without a word, she met her husband's gaze and walked away with her child.

Rage and confusion consumed her. Why could she never sense the trouble meant for her life? Was she destined never to find love or stability? Helplessness threatened to crush her, but her will to protect her daughter carried her forward. She drew breath with effort, forcing herself not to cry and awaken her sleeping child, anchoring herself in the warmth of her daughter pressed to her chest. Helplessness would not be her inheritance.

Fear, once a trembling shadow, she honed into a blade—eyes sweeping every alley, every street, every stranger for threat or chance. That same energy hardened into armor. She would teach Kebbeh not only to endure, but to see beyond the veil, to thrive where others faltered. In that moment, Ma Eliza knew her second sight was no mere gift—it was a burden of duty, a call to act, not simply to witness.

After what felt like two miles, she saw a vacancy sign above an auto shop. The owner, a kind young Lebanese man named Nabil, had just purchased the shop and offered her the apartment upstairs. She and Kebbeh slept on a pallet, saving for a bed, a dresser, and a small gold kerosene lamp.

"Chey," Ma Satta said, "that baby face is imprinted on your back for life, oh."

With a dry laugh, they shared a moment of comfort. The village of women gave her love, security, and strength. Maybe her second sight had been guiding her toward them all along.

Under the hot sun, beneath brightly colored umbrellas, the market women moved with rhythm and determination. Their dry hands prepared food, their quick tongues negotiated survival, their ears absorbed secrets. They were seen as background laborers by the country's elite, but they carried society on their backs.

Beatrice's personal driver, Peter Wilson, parked a block away from Dunbar General Market. She was seven months pregnant and enjoyed the walk. Her midwife had encouraged her to engage in daily movement to prevent her ankles from swelling.

Dressed in a dusty rose and turquoise embroidered kaftan with a matching head tie, gold clutch, and white sunglasses, she appeared nothing like a commoner. Yet she relished the brief fantasy of blending in. Vendors studied her with suspicion, unsure whether to welcome her or gossip once she left without buying.

Peter, a polite young engineering student, was grateful for the work. His salary from Boikai covered his tuition, room, and board. Wearing his uniform—black suit, tie, and gold lapel pin—made him feel important. But his duty extended beyond Beatrice. He also drove Boikai wherever he needed, never revealing his employer's movements to his wife.

That day, Beatrice was determined to visit Ma Eliza's stand. She knew Eliza was her husband's mistress's mother. Yet Ma Eliza remained cordial, never condoning Kebbeh's choices in public.

When Beatrice approached, Ma Eliza greeted her: "Good morning, Mrs. Collins, is baby giving you a hard time today?"

With a chuckle, Beatrice replied, "No, Ma, baby loves how much I walk. It lulls him to sleep."

Eliza asked, "You know if that is a boy growing in your belly?"

Beatrice said, "Who knows, Ma. This old ma in our house, washing our bedding, said, 'Dat boy.' I told her, How you know, old ma?"

"The old ma said, 'The way your face is still beautiful, a girl in your belly would make you look ugly.'"

The two women laughed together. For a moment, they shared solidarity—one who had borne a child long ago, and one about to become a mother.

The moment passed quickly when Ma Eliza said to Beatrice, "Kebbeh knows that she's having a boy, the way the baby kicks, he will be a footballer quick, oh.

"She so big, I told her she looks like she has a football club in there."

Beatrice's smile turned to fury. "Why would you say that woman's name in my presence? I beg you, I don't want to hear that woman's name!" she shouted.

The shoppers froze, waiting for the scene to unfold.

"Calm the hell down, small girl," Ma Eliza bellowed. "Kebbeh is my child. You better not disrespect my only child, so help me God! You either buy from my stand or pass your ass from me before that one inside gets born today!"

Beatrice threw three U.S. dollars in Eliza's face and snatched an orange. "Next time, if I come back here, don't say that woman's name again. Cut my orange and I will move from here!"

Eliza scored the orange with her knife and handed it back. Beatrice slurped it, tossed the rest at her, and stormed off.

Ma Eliza's scream burst through the air as Beatrice turned her back. "That baby in your womb will not make it! I know your fate." The words tore from her throat, raw and ragged, but in that instant her vision sharpened. Shadows spun like smoke around the unborn child, curling and shifting with the weight of things yet to come.

Was it destiny pressing upon her, or the red-hot anger of a mother betrayed? Her heart thundered, caught between fury's fire and the whisper of prophecy. For as long as she could remember, the sight had been both her beacon and her burden. It revealed what others could not bear to see and chained her to truths she could never fully master.

In that moment, it felt like a double-edged blade—gleaming with knowledge yet cutting her spirit with helplessness. Was she speaking as a woman scorned or as a vessel of fate? She could not tell.

Clenching her fists, Ma Eliza forced her breath steady. She vowed that if visions were to haunt her, she would wield them with purpose. No shadow, no prophecy, no curse of fate would decide the course of her daughter's life.

Beatrice paused, fear freezing her for an instant, before continuing to her driver.

Old Ma Satta, who sold onions from Paynesville, rushed to restrain Eliza. "Those people aren't worth the trouble," she begged. "Their day will come. Change is coming, oh. Don't force what is supposed to come."

A tear streaked down Eliza's face. Memories of how men had used her rose like bile, but she forced them down. Customers waited patiently. She picked up the bruised orange and scattered money, wiped her forehead with her headtie, and reset her voice.

"Five dollars for five oranges."

There was no time to carry those feelings. She had a grandson to prepare for and rent to pay.

Chapter 8: Peter

Open your eyes, my child. The water, air, ground, and music spirit will guide you through. The people are going to make a big palava. Look to God, who will see you through. Only He is in control and will await you back in His loving arms at that blessed time of His coming. His love is ubiquitous and deafening.

"That music is too loud, Peter, I beg you!" Beatrice snapped from the back of the family's black Cadillac.

The radio blared Funkadelic, and Peter wanted Benson Street to feel every note. This music was more than the new sound. It was the pulse of freedom, a world bigger than himself-bigger than the streets and the Collins family's constant demands. He ached for the sound to drown out the noise of his duty and a moment of resistance. "Beatrice, this is the sound of America! How can you not feel the groove?"

"I'm telling you, I want silence. If you want to groove, go to the dance hall. Let me ride in peace."

Peter sighed, turning the dial down, catching her glare in the rearview. "Yes, ma'am. Sorry, mah."

She folded her arms. "All I hear from you is this Funkadelic. What's the appeal?"

"It's the new sound—George Clinton and Parliament. A real jive, oh."

"It's too sexual for my taste."

Peter chuckled. "Some music is meant to be. That's how new generations get made."

Beatrice laughed hard. "You think our parents didn't have 'juke me' music to bring us here?" She shook her head. "Peter, you're too stupid, mehn."

There was something about the music and Peter's love of it—it was a way to make his boss's wife more comfortable around him. The drives would have been long and bumpy. Sometimes her nausea would take over, especially on unpaved roadways.

Peter felt that the bass of the radio or his eight-track would somehow distract her.

He could not afford to upset his only clients. The Collins family paid him so handsomely that they had installed a personal telephone in his dormitory, a line that rang only for them. At first, the gift had thrilled him. None of his classmates had such a luxury. But soon the constant calls became chains, their voices on the other end pulling him away from the lecture hall, from the library, from the world of ideas he had once fought so hard to reach.

Each ring reminded him that his loyalty was bought and bound. Answering meant comfort, security, and the promise of money his family needed. Ignoring it meant betrayal—not only of the Collinses, but of his elder brother, the one who had trusted him with the recommendation.

Yet every answered call came at the cost of his education. His professors were disappointed at his empty seat, his incomplete projects stacked like silent assignments on his desk. Once, he had sketched bridges on the backs of napkins while waiting for Beatrice or Boikai to finish their errands—his mind alive with designs, the kind of ambition that made his heart race. Now, those sketches teased him, reminders of the path slipping further from his grasp.

He told himself he could manage both—the demands of his benefactors and the rigor of the university. But each day the scales tipped heavier toward obligation, while his ambition grew lighter, like a dream fading in daylight. Between loyalty and longing, he felt himself stretched thin, torn between being the man his family relied upon and the scholar he still yearned to become.

Beatrice would call Peter daily and urge him, "It's too important, and you are the only one I can count on."

Peter's eyes locked with hers, and he was happy to oblige. Mrs. Beatrice liked her routine. Sunday, church service, then to the market. On Monday, she preferred to go to the clinic and the library. Tuesdays and Wednesdays, she loved spending time with her girlfriends at their houses right after the men left for work. They played 21 and gossiped. Friday, she volunteered at the all-girls boarding house, and Saturday, she visited her mother at her childhood home.

No matter how busy her days seemed, she moved like a lonely machine, wound tight and set in motion for others. Every interaction was wrapped in a sigh, a quiet echo that said she kept trying, oh. She wore the face of high society, polished and poised, yet underneath, she bent to everyone's needs but her own. Trained by her parents to serve, she now served her husband. A wife, after all, was not meant to sit quietly at home. No, she had to be educated, visible, carrying God's charge as a dutiful wife, obedient daughter, faithful spouse.

And Boikai—he never granted her respect. In the car, his voice struck down like stones: "You're late," or "Hush your mouth." Always cutting, never kind.

At the dance hall, Boikai lingered too long, reeking of Kebbeh's perfume, and when he returned, he was not alone. Kebbeh slipped in beside him, their laughter tangled, their bodies careless in the backseat. And there he sat at the wheel, silent, steady, eyes fixed on the road, carrying them all home while swallowing what should never be his to bear.

Two months later, Kebbeh whispered her news to Boikai in the backseat of his Blue Monte Carlo: she was pregnant. His face lit with excitement, but a shadow quickly followed, a look that told her this pregnancy would not be his escape from Beatrice.

In a hush heavy with dread, he said, "So is Beatrice."

The words settled between them, heavier than the air. They turned their eyes to the horizon, where the grey clouds split for the sunset. Fingers entwined, they stared out at the restless ocean. The waves beat against the shore and their feet, warning of what was to come—swift, relentless, and painful.

Peter watched the couple drift further down the beach. The waves crashing against the black rocks spoke more clearly than they did, confirming what he already knew: life as it was would soon fracture.

Boikai was riddled with guilt. In Liberian society, it was not considered taboo for a man to have children by different mothers at the same time. Still, he knew Beatrice would never accept Kebbeh's child in their lives. Her jealous rage toward the woman she felt most threatened by—now carrying another child by her husband—burned hotter than ever.

One rainy July evening, Peter spotted Beatrice outside the mechanic shop, standing beneath a lamppost and screaming for

Kebbeh to come out and fight her. Peter rushed forward, grabbed her, and forced her back into the Cadillac before driving off.

Their trial had already begun. The wedding of the century loomed just a month away. How was a new reporter supposed to keep her composure when the man she loved was vowing himself to someone else?

The weekly drives fell into silence. After the market quarrel between Mrs. Beatrice and Ma Eliza, Monrovia buzzed with scandal. The car became a tomb—Beatrice refusing the radio, refusing even the sound of Peter's breath.

Hours later, when they reached her mother's country house, she finally broke the silence. "I've known about Kebbeh all along."

Her voice did not waver. "This is my bed, and I must lie in it. I don't need your sympathy, your pity, or your disgust. One day, that husband of mine will falter, and when he does, I need you ready to take me and my child to the airport."

Peter's reply was barely audible. "Mrs. Beatrice, you can't leave the country without your husband's consent."

She met his eyes, and in one quick breath, she said, "You think I don't know that? That's why tomorrow, at the American Embassy, you will pretend to be my husband.

"The Americans don't know who you are."

"Ma'am, in good conscience, I cannot betray Boikai."

Peter could not afford to deceive his boss in that way. He did not want to be charged with a crime, even though he felt pity for her; the risk was too high for him to agree.

"Peter," Beatrice's voice cut through the silence, low and trembling with fury, "you've been betraying me since the day we hired you. How many times did you pick that woman up, carry her to this very car, to have sex with my husband… only to drive me in the morning as if nothing happened? Do they all think I am so blind? So stupid?"

Her hand pressed against her stomach; her voice stung. "I need to leave this man here and start a new life—with my child."

The car rolled to a halt at the iron gate of her mother's country estate. Peter climbed out, the weight of her words piercing him like thorns. He lifted the gate, each groan of metal grinding against his chest, and drove through. When he rounded to her side and opened the door, Beatrice stepped out with a cold demeanor. Their eyes locked, hers fierce with desperation, his bridled with guilt.

She leaned closer, her voice breaking into a whisper meant only for him. "I'm begging you…you owe me that much."

Tears burned Peter's eyes as he turned away, torn in two. Discernment and strife warred in his chest as he walked back to the driver's seat. He gripped the wheel, knuckles white, the silence in the car heavier than any music could fill.

His thoughts drifted to Aunty Celeste, who had begged him to help her escape her abusive husband with their three-year-old son. She had pleaded with her nephew to sign the papers that would allow her boy to leave for Belgium. But when Peter arrived at the embassy, he saw one of his uncle's friends sitting at the desk. Shaken with fear, he turned and ran before he could act.

A week later, they found his aunt and her son washed ashore in the Baptism River.

For two hours, he wrestled with his thoughts: should he honor Beatrice's plea and help her escape, or betray her trust by warning Boikai of her plan? The memory of what had happened to Aunty Celeste and her son haunted him—he could not let such a fate befall Beatrice.

Boikai was unfaithful, yes, but he was not an abusive man. *They will be alright*, Peter told himself. Beatrice could leave him and still remain in Liberia. In the end, he convinced himself it was a matter between husband and wife, no matter how desperate her plea had been.

The road stretched ahead, long and merciless, carrying him toward Kebbeh's apartment. She was in labor. And Peter, bound by secrets on every side, drove on—his silence the only witness to a storm about to break.

Chapter 9: Fula

The sweetness of a mother lay in the milk she gave her child at birth, which nourished her baby, fortifying her child's strength. The grains of the African soil were intertwined with each daughter of the land they called home. Those grains of soil embedded themselves in a mother's will, and the scars of her fear, doubt, and joy stitched themselves into the hearts of her children and generations thereafter. When the stitches unraveled, would true healing commence?

"Fula! Mehn, wake up!!" The young girl awoke from a deep slumber. Her mother was overjoyed—her daughter was about to have the opportunity of a lifetime. She would be the house girl for one of the most influential families in the country.

Fula was just shy of ten years old when her mother, Maggie, told her she was to live in the home of a family she had never met. Maggie sold dried cod at the market next to Ma Eliza and had overheard from one of the patrons that Boikai and Beatrice were expecting a baby and would need help looking after the child and caring for the house.

Maggie didn't hesitate to jump at the chance. With Fula working for the Collinses, they could finally move closer to Benson Street—and their child would be in the presence of the most powerful people in the country. Maggie boasted that her eldest child would be the best candidate to "mind the baby" for the new family.

Fula loved science. She wanted to become a chemist. She used to mix different types of soaps and fragrances, trying to create her dresses to smell like cloves and passion fruit. She didn't know that the choices her mother made would never allow her to pursue that dream. She was about to be forced into a very uncomfortable situation—one she would have to bury deep inside, carrying the burden of that secret for the rest of her life.

Lying on her pallet between her three small brothers, she sat up, her three plaits pointing atop her head like a compass. Half-asleep, she began packing her small knapsack. Her mother, with anxious breath, spoke in a quiet authority, laying out the rules for how to act in front of her new employers.

"You are to do whatever they tell you—no talking back, no questioning. You are to pay attention to the baby, bathe her, wash her bottles, wash her clothes, and feed her."

"Mommy, should I pack my school uniform? My school will be much closer now that I will be in Monrovia."

Her mother looked at her in dismay. "For what? You will get back to school when that baby goes to school."

From that eerie morning on, Fula's dream of becoming a chemist withered. Her new duty was to care for a baby she did not know, in a family that was not her own.

She closed her eyes and pressed her back against the rough cinderblock wall, letting herself drift into the life she once imagined. In her mind, she was a grown woman standing proudly in a shop with her name etched above the door: Fula's Fragrances. Sunlight spilled over glass bottles scattered across a wicker table, each one labeled in her careful hand.

But the vision shattered. She saw herself hurling the vials onto the street, glass exploding against the stone. With a scream, she knew deep in her soul that the dream was gone.

Still, she reached for her hand broom, sweeping the shards into the gutter, watching the fragrances trickle away with the dust and rainwater. No one would see her weakness—a child in pain. She became the strength she needed in that moment to work and provide for her family. What was once childhood was no more; she had a deep obligation to her mother and to this new child she was yet to meet and protect.

While her mother ironed her Sunday school dress, Fula bathed herself and rubbed on her lotion made of shea butter and jasmine oil. She wanted to look nice for her new home. She was terrified to leave her family behind. Her siblings, still restless in bed, didn't wake to say their goodbyes.

Her father had died in a tragic construction accident. He was working on a bridge, but wasn't properly secured. He drowned with three others just shy of her fifth birthday. His Drakkar Noir cologne was seared into her memory. Maybe that's when her fascination with scents began—trying to recreate his smell. Maybe that would bring her father back.

Watching her mother scurry around their one-bedroom apartment, connected to a fabric store on Old Tubman Road, Fula put on her navy blue cotton dress with silver buttons and a yellow ribbon belt. Her mother fixed her hair and tied yellow ribbons to her braids, calming the plaits back down to earth.

"Look, their driver will pick you up. Go wait outside the shop. Go now, my dear. This will help our family so much, oh. I don't want to hear no trouble. The money you get will help us so much."

"Okay, Mommy."

Fula shyly left the only home she had ever known and waited outside on Old Tubman Road for the driver.

Peter pulled up to Harrod's Fabric Emporium and saw a young girl dressed in her best, holding a red and blue plastic grocery bag. He stepped out of the Cadillac, greeted Fula, and drove her to the Collins house. She was so nervous to leave the home that she knew the reason for her being there, but still felt out of place.

When they arrived, Fula saw Boikai and Beatrice arguing in the kitchen.

"Boikai, this baby doesn't feel right," Beatrice said. "She won't nurse, and she keeps screaming in pain."

Boikai shook his head. "You're just exhausted, Beatrice. How can you say that? This child is yours. You gave birth to her—I was there."

Beatrice sharply screamed back, "No, you weren't! By the time I awoke, you were there with a broken hand, and you still won't tell me what the hell happened!"

Peter cleared his throat.

The look on their faces shifted to surprise. Fula, hiding behind Peter, braced herself—afraid she was about to get slapped for eavesdropping.

Peter slid over to introduce the new employee. "This is Fula," he said. "She's Maggie's child—the one you asked for to help mind the baby."

Beatrice wiped the fear from her eyes to a quick face of poise and authority. She glanced at Fula and handed her a dry cloth diaper. "Go change the baby," she said, motioning to the back hallway where baby Joviah was sleeping.

With a deep breath, Fula walked down the hall and stepped into the biggest bedroom she had ever seen. The floor gleamed with polished marble tiles. The crib, made of acacia wood, had yellow-painted stripes along its columns. The changing table was white wicker, with glass bottles that clinked together when moved.

She looked like a little butterfly inside her crib. Her hair looked like small tufts of black sheep wool. When she looked at Joviah, she felt an unexplainable joy.

Fula sweetly said, "Good morning, little butterfly."

Baby Joviah kicked her feet, looked up at Fula, and responded to her voice.

Fula smiled as she picked up Joviah, who wriggled in her arms. She whispered, *I will call you Little Butterfly.* Like the bright butterflies that had danced around her mother's pepper bushes back home, a reminder that even in hard times, God gives a tender surprise—fragile, yet full of promise.

From that day on, Fula knew: this baby was her primary responsibility. She would take care of this butterfly.

Back in the kitchen, Boikai leaned against the counter. "Beatrice, my woman, you're still weak from childbirth. No wonder you don't feel yourself. It'll pass. Just be patient."

Beatrice's voice cut sharply. "I know my body, Boikai. I blacked out from high blood pressure—and the next thing I remember, a baby was on my chest. But this feeling… this baby doesn't feel like mine."

His jaw clenched. He slammed his fist against the kitchen table, the sound echoing through the room. "You're thinking too much! This foolishness of yours must stop. That is your child. I was there when they laid her on you. You fainted from the pain—nothing more. She's yours."

He jabbed a finger toward her, voice rising. "Now close your mouth before it says something it should never dare to speak!"

Then the silence came thick, oppressive. And in that stillness, Boikai knew. He had to guard the lie. Because if the truth surfaced, both his worlds—Kebbeh's and Beatrice's—would shatter beyond repair.

Months passed, and Fula settled into the rhythm of the house. Each morning, she scrubbed the floors before the baby stirred. In the evenings, she washed the tiny clothes and hung them neatly on the line, imagining they belonged to the doll baby she had always longed for.

Fula leaned against the crib, her arms heavy as she watched the baby's chest rise and fall. The soft sound of her breathing filled the room, and for a moment, she felt something like pride—this tiny life needed her. But beneath that moment swelled an emptiness she couldn't shake. No one had ever asked what she wanted, what she dreamed of. No one congratulated her or validated her work.

Every bottle she warmed, every cloth she washed, every powder she pressed into the child's skin seemed to vanish into silence—her labor seen, but her heart unseen. Still, she pulled herself upright, tightened the ribbons in her hair as if they could hold her together, and whispered to the shadows, *I am alright, oh. I am alright.*

When the baby awoke, Fula bathed her in the pink tub. The scent of black soap filled the room as she worked the lather into the towel, then gently washed the child's small body. She even knew the perfect time to powder her from head to toe—just as the heat began to rise—so the powder would absorb her sweat. Fula would pour her favorite shea butter, scented with jasmine oil, all over the baby so she could shine in the sun.

Little Butterfly was starting to hop on two feet, trying to climb out of her crib. That same yellow crib with stripes was getting worn from baby Joviah kicking her strong feet on the slats. Fula would lift her up over the crib and play with her on the blanket on the floor. She would sing songs and clap, saying, "Flutter, our butterfly, flutter!"

And Joviah would smile her gummy smile.

Fula loved this life. All she had to do was take care of the baby and sleep in her own bedroom.

Even Miss Beatrice got Fula her favorite scents at the market to make her little potions and fragrances. She even asked Mrs. Beatrice to go with her to the market to find the correct herbs and flowers she could use.

Shortly after Sunday Mass, Fula was washing the baby's clothes outside. While scrubbing the cloth diapers in the soapy bucket, she overheard Peter and Boikai arguing in hushed tones. "Your conscience will never be whole, Mr. Boikai. Your wife needs to know that the child is not hers," said Peter.

Boikai, pacing back and forth with his driver with clenched fists, sucked his teeth and said to Peter, "I owe you my explanation?! You better fix your mouth. She's too fragile to know. Joviah is our child, no matter how she got her. Take me to Kebbeh. I need to see my other child."

Peter shook his head in disappointment and complied. He locked eyes with his boss and said sternly, "Yes, sir," and drove Boikai to Kebbeh's apartment.

Fula stayed along the wall underneath the clothesline. She dropped the cloth diapers in her hand. She dropped down in fear that the men might have spotted her. She was in shock over what she had just heard. Watching their feet enter the garage, Fula took a deep breath, a mix of fear and the knowledge of the truth.

How could she face Mrs. Beatrice? Where was Joviah's real mother? Would she be sent back home to her mother if she told Mrs. Beatrice the truth?

Christmas came in a somber face. Mrs. Beatrice gifted Fula a mortar and pestle made of pink soapstone. It even had her initials carved on the side—"F.R." for Fula Roberts. Fula felt like a big-time chemist. She couldn't wait to mix new fragrances that she would find around town.

The months stretched to bitterness on February 12, 1981, just as dusk fell. There was an eerie stillness around the house. No motorbikes zipped up and down the avenue. No neighbors gossiping on porches. Even the crickets seemed to hush. The silence pressed in on them, thick and unnatural. People were too afraid to step outside.

Boikai was downtown working at the government office. Beatrice was in her room, humming hymns under her breath as her needle pierced the white satin fabric on Joviah's baptismal gown. Peter lounged in the front room, watching Manchester United on television, his face reflecting the blue glow of the screen while the crowd's distant roar sounded oddly out of place in their hushed street.

Fula crouched in the bathroom, bathing Joviah in her little pink tub. Bubbles rose around them. The scent of black soap clung to her hands. The baby's slippery body wriggled in her caretaker's arms, warm water cascading down the tiled floor.

This was not a typical Thursday evening. This was a night etched into Fula's memory forever. Every evening, they followed the same routine. Curfew rang its invisible bell at 6:00 p.m. sharp. Commander Dolay—now calling himself Liberia's new president—made sure his people feared the dark. Feared stepping past their doorsteps. Feared even the flicker of light through a window. He taught them to shut it all out: close the curtains, bolt the shutters, hide from the world. Because if his soldiers caught sight of light after curfew, they shot first. Questions were for corpses.

But that night, there was something heavier in the air. The stillness wasn't safety. It was waiting. It was a warning.

BAM!

The front door exploded open with a splintering crack. The vibration rattled the bathroom door, and Fula's heart slammed against her ribs.

Foday Freeman stood there, flanked by two soldiers. His uniform reeked of sweat and cigarettes, his eyes wild with revenge. He had traded his mechanic's life for the life of a freedom soldier. He had finally felt the lure of the new president, Dolay, who promised power and vengeance to those who joined his cause.

"Where is Boikai!?"

Peter collapsed to the floor as if his knees had given way, both hands raised. His lips trembled, but no sound came.

Bang! Another shot tore through the air. "Please, my man, I beg you—" Peter crumpled, blood pooling fast. The television kept blaring, the roar of the match commentators grotesquely cheerful.

In the bathroom, Fula froze, water dripping down her arms as she clutched the baby to her chest. Joviah's skin felt hot against her grip, slick from soap, her tiny fists thrashing. She whimpered, and Fula pressed her tighter, praying she wouldn't cry.

But the sounds in the next room shattered any prayer: the heavy thud of boots striking flesh. Peter's strangled cry. Foday's roar:

"Where the fuck is Boikai?! He owes me an explanation, Peter!"

"I beg you, sir—I don't know where he is—" Peter's voice was thin, choking.

"You're lying!" Foday barked, the words sharp as gunfire. "You're his driver! You know where he goes!"

"I swear—I don't—"

The sound of bodies colliding with walls. Then a metallic click. Fula's blood went cold. She dropped to her knees, words spilling out—half-prayer, half-sob. "Papa God… is this how I die? Is this what my mother sent me for—to look after a baby that would bring my death?"

Foday yanked Peter up by the arm and pressed a gun under his chin. His voice was a growl, a death sentence: "If you lie—you die. If you tell the truth—you die. So what's it going to be?"

Joviah let out a cry. Fula's arms trembled as she tried to quiet her, rocking on the wet floor, the towel sliding loose. She peed herself in fear, warm liquid seeping down her legs, mixing with bathwater.

The first soldier, Clarence, barged into the bathroom. The stink of alcohol clung to him. His shadow filled the doorway.

"Where's the man of the house?!"

Fula trembled, soaked, reeking of soap, urine, and smoke. She cradled Joviah, naked and wailing now. Her voice cracked to a whisper. "I don't know, sir. I'm just the house girl. I only take care of the baby."

He sneered, eyes glinting. "Baby you takin' care of? Let's see how you do that when there's no food." He stormed toward the kitchen. Pots clattered, cupboards slammed. Then Beatrice's scream.

Fula stumbled to the doorway and saw Beatrice pinned against the wall, her nightgown damp with sweat, a rifle shoved beneath her breast. Her trembling hands still clutched the half-sewn baptismal gown.

The other soldier ransacked the shelves, smashing plates to shards, until his hand closed on the can of Similac. His laugh was hollow. He carried it outside, popped his lighter, and within seconds the powdery formula was a plume of black smoke. The pungent scent burned Fula's nostrils as he spat into the flame.

"Hmm, da baby got bad luck, oh."

Fula screamed, thrusting Joviah into Beatrice's arms, then darted outside with her little pink mortar and pestle. Kneeling in the dirt, she scraped desperately at the ashes, scooping whatever powder remained. The smoke stung her eyes. Her hands shook. How would this child survive?

When Fula stumbled back inside, Foday had Peter pinned to the wall again, the barrel of his pistol digging into his temple.

"Where is Boikai?!"

Peter's blood glistened under the flicker of the TV. Fula's chest heaved with fury and terror.

Foday laughed, a cruel, echoing sound. He looked at Beatrice and shouted, "Take your shit and get out!"

The lady of the house and her house girl scrambled. One suitcase. Whatever their hands touched, they grabbed. Beatrice wrapped Joviah in the unfinished baptismal gown. Fula clutched her pink mortar and pestle as though it could save them.

And they ran. Into the night. Into fear. The last piercing gunshot bellowed from the house; they knew Peter was gone. They had no time to react; they had to run straight to Beatrice's parents' house.

Where was Boikai? Not at work. Not protecting them. He was at Kebbeh's, playing with baby James.

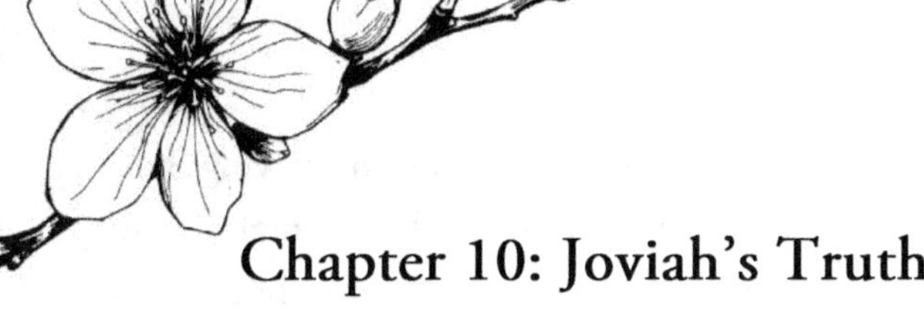

Chapter 10: Joviah's Truth

The Lone Star had fallen, not from the sky, but from grace—and only time would unveil the full weight of its descent. As society collapsed beneath betrayal, even the Honorable Ones now knelt at the mercy of rebel hands that held power without justice.

The sounds of sirens, gunshots, and harrowing screams competed with each other in the cold, dark night. Beatrice, Fula, and baby Joviah stayed at her parents' home, having narrowly escaped Foday and his rebels. To send a message, the insurgents had burned the Collins' house to the ground.

Boikai slept in his office intermittently and sometimes at Kebbeh's apartment. Foday had placed a bounty on his head. Beatrice's rage in the aftermath of Peter's killing left her unwilling to engage with her philandering husband. Punishing Boikai for not being there—for spending time with his mistress and their child—was too glaring to ignore.

Beatrice's detachment from Joviah persisted. Her mother said it was normal to feel sadness after giving birth, yet Joviah was nearly one, and still, there was no bond. At night, when the house sank into silence, Beatrice cradled Joviah against her chest, studying the child's face. The lashes curled like Boikai's; the widow's peak mirrored Kebbeh's. In those moments, Beatrice felt both mother and thief, rocking a child who had never truly been hers.

Sometimes she hummed lullabies through clenched teeth, daring herself to believe love might bloom if she sang long enough. But it never came. What filled her instead was an ache that hollowed her chest—a wound without blood, without name.

How could there be? Joviah was not truly hers. She belonged to Kebbeh. Beatrice's own baby had slipped away in his sleep, their sweet angel boy who never saw another day. No one predicted that she, too, would be marked by the same sorrow that once claimed her mother, yet the pattern unfolded, as if fate itself refused to loosen its grip.

The beautiful, nightmarish day left Beatrice's face swollen until her reflection seemed unrecognizable. Headaches followed—pounding behind her eyes, her vision blurred as though time itself had stalled. She drifted into sleep, her body betraying its purpose. Eclampsia did not arrive graciously; it struck like an old curse, seizing womb and mind with relentless hands. Sorrow moved through bloodlines the way waterfalls carve the earth. She carried the grief of generations before her, only to be awakened by a beautiful, angelic stranger on her breast.

Kebbeh gave birth to twins, James and Joviah. She and Boikai agreed to give Joviah to Beatrice, as long as the child stayed with her father. Foday was convinced the children were his, which drove his obsession to track down and kill Boikai—and raise the children himself. Kebbeh knew the dangerous price she paid for having two lovers. Deep down, she knew who her children's father was, but the secret would stay with her until her dying breath.

Boikai promised Kebbeh that he would keep their daughter in the country, so she could watch her little girl grow up before her eyes. Kebbeh was pleased—her daughter would have a better life than she had. The truth could not be revealed, or the family's downfall would ripple through generations.

Two weeks after Peter's killing, Beatrice contemplated leaving Boikai once and for all.

"Let it be so, Beatrice," said her mother, Josephine. "You've been crying for two weeks, my child. Are you going to leave Boikai, or are you and that man going to move to America?"

"Ma, I don't know." Beatrice's voice cracked. "Seeing Peter get shot point-blank in front of me... and that rebel asking for my husband. What does he want with Boikai?"

"I don't even know where Boikai is.

"And don't say that woman's name in this house, Ma!" Beatrice snapped, her voice sharp and unrelenting. The name Kebbeh pulled something primal from her.

She knew in her heart her husband was with her. And in some small, desperate place, she hoped that holding Joviah in her arms would be enough to bring him home—to keep him from going back. Who wanted to be a failure in a marriage, not even a year old? A single mother, with a baby not hers by blood, in a country collapsing on itself.

But Beatrice had a plan: she would leave for America with her baby girl and start over. Whether Boikai followed or not, she didn't care. She refused to let her daughter grow up in a country where rights were stripped away daily. Inflation had turned survival into chaos. The line between rich and poor was gone— everyone was scrambling for rice, oil, dignity. Even clergymen, politicians, and family friends were begging or dying in the streets.

It numbed the soul.

It was hell on earth.

And still, people waited for justice, as if it were a sunrise that never came.

October 1981 arrived quietly, one still night that seemed to know what it was hiding. Beatrice, Boikai, and Joviah packed a green valise and set out for the United States of America.

Fula bowed at Beatrice's feet, begging her to take her with them. "Mrs. Beatrice, I beg you, mehn. Please—there is nothing for me here. I need to help with the baby, or I'll be a good girl and go to school. I'm so sorry, ma. I'll be good, oh. I can't stay here. My ma is gone. My brothers are gone. You are my people. I beg you! Please, God, I beg!"

Beatrice lifted Fula from the ground, her body limp with fear of abandonment, tilted her chin until their eyes met, and said, "My child, I will send for you when we get settled.

"Thank you for taking care of our Joviah.

"I will reach for you. Don't worry."

Fula stood on the veranda of Beatrice's parents' home and watched her future drive away. Deep down in her soul, she knew Beatrice would not keep her promise. That was the day her heart turned toward spiteful revenge—for when you have nothing to lose, you can do the unthinkable.

Time does not heal all wounds; it carries them forward, shape-shifting into new generations. Thirty years later, in Paris, Joviah unveiled her third *Bridal by Jovi* fashion show. The African Queen was the talk of designers and editors worldwide. The top

Black supermodels would be featured. For the first time, her father would attend.

"Your dad is proud of you, Jovi," said Henry. "It's hard for him to cheer for you. He feels like he failed in his own life."

"That's bullshit and you know it," said Joviah. "He's just disappointed the son he never had has this much success."

"Well, let's prove him wrong like you always do." The gleam of excitement in Henry's smile gave Joviah the validation she still searched for. What she never received from her father, she received in her love's encouragement.

"He's excited because he'll be hearing Sade perform during the show," said Joviah.

The crowd buzzed. Top celebrities in the bridal fashion world were in attendance—including Paola Avant, the Anna Wintour of *Bridal Vogue*. She had flown in from her flat in Milan just to see another Jovi couture show. Paola had given Jovi her first big break after graduating from FIT, taking her on as an intern. Jovi's style was eccentric—always nodding to her African roots—but something was not quite whole.

The audience was about to discover her ultimate vision.

The finale gown was a masterwork of heritage and couture: sculpted from upcycled rice-bag burlap, shimmering with hand-sewn cowry-shell beading and a constellation of Swarovski crystals. A sixteen-foot cape trailed behind, painted with the luminous faces of her two grandmothers and her mother, bordered with orange blossoms. It was not just a showstopper; it was an anthem. Joviah felt the power of an African Empress. She felt the spirit of her grandmothers on that stage, their excellence already ingrained in her DNA. Nothing and no one could spoil this joyful accomplishment she had created for herself. When Joviah dreamed of African queens, these women were her eternal muse.

Backstage, her hands trembled as she smoothed the hem of the finale gown. Beyond the curtain, the roar of the crowd rose and fell like a distant heartbeat, yet inside her chest every pulse thundered with expectation—not only her own, but those of spirits lingering in her blood: a father who had doubted her, a mother who had grieved what could never be, two women whose strength had carved the path beneath her feet, and a husband who looked to her for inspiration and love.

This gown was more than fabric and silk. It was defiance stitched into every seam, reclamation shimmering with each bead. It was her declaration: she could honor the past without being bound to it.

As the models filed into place, her reflection caught in the mirrored wall—elegant, unshakable, every line of her face composed. Yet behind the mask, her nerves coiled tighter, whispering of the prices already paid: the questions left unanswered, the scars no one else could see. The runway ahead gleamed like a promise, but with every step, she knew she would carry the shadow of family secrets that no spotlight could ever erase.

Couture Trina, a popular wedding blogger, had long been a critic. "How can a Liberian fashion designer make wedding gowns when she hasn't even been back to her own country for inspiration?" she once posted. "Fraud much?"

Joviah made sure Couture Trina sat right next to Paola—front and center—to choke on her words.

She had spent ten years researching fabrics for each African region, aiming to celebrate a woman on her wedding day. She infused American silhouettes with the fingerprints of fabrics across the continent—a nod and a prayer to the land that gave her life and continued to call her home.

This was her father's first visit to any of her shows. He hadn't attended her debut at the Harlem Boys & Girls Club when she was twenty-three. He'd said fashion was just a hobby, not a real career. So Joviah made sure this time he sat beside Vera Wang and Vivienne Westwood.

Her parents had divorced two years ago. The silence in that Michigan home had grown unbearable. Beatrice had since moved to Paris, into an apartment overlooking the Eiffel Tower.

The energy of the show was electric. Sade opened with *"Your Love Is King."* Models with natural hair—Bantu knots, cornrows, afros—adorned with gold jewelry and luminous makeup glided down the runway to the harmonies of bongos, saxophones, and Sade's sultry melodies.

Looking backstage, Joviah peeked into the audience and saw her father seated beside another woman. They were holding hands. Something about her smile felt familiar.

Across the stage, Joviah saw her mother with an older American man. They laughed together, easy and intimate. It wasn't surprising her parents had moved on, but why today—her day? Her heart clenched. Their happiness once again overshadowed her success. She smiled for the cameras, but inside she felt hollow.

During the show, Beatrice spotted Kebbeh seated beside Boikai. Their eyes locked. After nearly thirty years, the two women stood in the same space—no shadows, no secrets. Beatrice felt it like a knife: the third person in her marriage had won.

Kebbeh mouthed across the room: "He's mine now."

Beatrice's eyes sharpened. She mouthed back: "Stupid woman."

They held each other's gaze so long they barely noticed the show had ended—until thunderous applause broke their trance.

The after-party glowed on a rooftop terrace, sponsored by a luxury wedding magazine. Joviah and Henry mingled while her parents remained separated—together in space, oceans apart in spirit. Boikai strolled over and gave Jovi a stiff hug.

"Great show, my darling," he said. "Didn't know you had it in you."

With a dry smile, she replied, "Of course, Dad. You never had faith in me."

He scowled. "You better stop this foolishness and take the damn compliment."

"If that's the best you can do, I'll take it."

He forced a grin, then gestured to his guest. "Joviah, meet Aunty Kebbeh."

"Aunty?" she blinked. "Wait—she's your sister?"

"No, dummy. She's my friend. You know better than to use someone's first name like that," he barked. "Respect your elders."

Joviah stared him down. "My apologies. Hello, Aunty Kebbeh." With a pinched grin, she walked away, disgusted. Henry handed her champagne.

"This man has the nerve to come to my event and call me a dummy over his little girlfriend?" Joviah snapped.

Henry pointed across the terrace. "Jovi… your mom's not too happy either."

They turned just in time to see Beatrice slap Kebbeh across the face. A gasp rippled through the crowd. Cameras flashed.

Boikai shouted, "Beatrice! How dare you—we're not even married anymore!"

He stormed off with Kebbeh in tow. Beatrice paused, gathered herself, and clinked glasses with a stranger, moving on as though nothing had happened.

"What the hell was that?" Joviah demanded.

"She's none of your concern," Beatrice said coolly. Thirty years of revenge flickered in her eyes like sweet vindication.

"She?" Jovi pressed.

"Kebbeh," Beatrice spat. "That woman should've stayed in history."

Kebbeh fled the party, the sting of the slap still burning. Boikai ran after her through the Paris streets.

"I can't live like this anymore, Boikai!" she cried.

"You need to tell our children the truth! They've been apart too long. They don't even know each other exists.

"And then you make my child call me Aunty Kebbeh? Don't mess with my intelligence!

"They're both thirty years old! They have a right to know, Boikai!"

Rain poured as they ducked beneath a closed café's awning. There, in the quiet storm, they made a plan to tell their twins the truth. Trembling, Boikai looked into Kebbeh's eyes and drew a deep breath. The lie that had bound them was breaking. He stopped in his tracks, shoulders sagging beneath the downpour. Rain matted his hair to his forehead, streamed into his eyes, but he made no move to wipe it away. He drew in another breath and let it out hollow, as though the years of weighted secrets themselves were spilling from his lungs.

Everything he had built—all the polished façades, the carefully buried truths—wavered like a house of cards in the storm. His hands shook, useless, betraying what he had spent a lifetime denying: he could no longer hold it all together.

A bitter laugh slipped from his throat, sharp and joyless. "Hmm… maybe they deserve the truth," he whispered, his voice stern against the rain. The words tasted like hot ash, burning with the knowledge that once spoken, there would be no gathering them back. He was willing to face the consequences. The pressures of what had been were no longer relevant.

"I will tell our daughter in the morning," Boikai said softly.

"It's best if it comes from me—her father.

"I set this hurricane of lies in motion. It's up to me to finally put it to rest." He kissed the love of his life and walked back to his hotel.

The cobblestones were slick from rain. The air smelled of rebirth, the truth ready to surface. Shivering in his wool overcoat, Boikai dialed Beatrice's number, ready to confess the secret of the child she had never met.

He stepped into an alley. A speeding police vehicle struck him down.

Boikai died instantly on the wet cobblestones overlooking the Seine.

On the other end of the line, Beatrice's scream pierced the silence.

Chapter 11:
Nobody Knows Tomorrow

Difficult choices drifted like whispers through the soul, quiet yet heavy, each one teetering on the edge of fate—each one capable of carving consequences that could not be undone.

Joviah knew her father was gone before she got the call. That night, after their quarrel on the rooftop in Paris, she had dreamt of him—dressed in an all-white suit, adorned with his Liberian country cloth. The black-and-white striped shirt, the fabric hat tilted gently toward the earth.

Beside him stood a grown man in a matching white suit, smiling, his hand resting on her father's shoulder. She heard her father's favorite song, *"Aki Special,"* in her head. The lyrics—"Nobody knows tomorrow"—echoed like a soft truth. The same lyrics they had sung and danced to in their living room back in their first apartment in Michigan. The way the man she had called Daddy would shake his hips to the rhythm while she spun in circles wearing her pink plastic jelly shoes, caked with dirt from outside. That song—their bond, their shared quiet moments of resting her head on his chest, feeling the bass beat through him. She pressed her hands to his face, tracing his scruffy beard, wishing she could go back in time. Wishing she had demanded answers, wishing their last conversation could have been peaceful, wishing she could undo the past that would never excuse her.

The bass of that song lulled her into the deepest sleep she had had in years. Daddy looked at peace. They said if you shared a strong bond with someone in this life, their spirit would visit you in your dreams. The veil between two souls always found a meeting place in the subconscious.

When she awoke to the terrible news, their favorite song became her song of regret.

Regret that their last conversation had been a stupid fight.

Regret for all things unsaid.

Regret for learning about her identity too late.

Regret for not cussing him out when she found out her truth. This song—once a bond between father and daughter—would now forever echo with betrayal. Because the man she knew was never the man who had raised her. That man had kept her from her flesh and blood her whole life, never offering a reason to reveal her truth while he was alive.

At the hospital, Beatrice got the frantic call from Joviah and rushed to the emergency room. She found Kebbeh sitting in the coroner's lobby, inconsolable, her son James by her side. James looked at her, confused. Kebbeh's guilt overtook her composure. Her lips pursed in anger. She knew that her ally in secrets had abandoned her to reap the consequences of their actions so long ago.

"Ma, why are you so upset? I know you saw him last, but it's Uncle Boikai. The last time you saw him was five years ago. I knew he was your boyfriend—it wasn't a secret," he said.

Kebbeh looked at him, her eyes tired and distant. "Don't be so naive, my child," she replied softly. "Boikai was your father."

James was left stunned in the hospital lobby as Kebbeh walked away. Joviah rushed in with her husband, Henry. They asked to speak with the coroner.

"Are you the next of kin?" the coroner asked. Trying to muster up her high school French, Joviah complied with the instructions. James looked at her—really looked at her. She looked like him. Like the female version of himself. And in his spirit, he knew: she was the missing piece he had been frantically searching for.

He didn't reveal himself to the beautiful stranger in that moment. She was too grief-stricken to process any more news she wasn't prepared for. Instead, he introduced himself simply as Kebbeh's son.

Henry recognized him immediately. "Wow. Small world. I didn't think I'd meet the all-star Parisian footballer at the hospital," he said, stunned.

The coroner asked Joviah to identify her father's body. The walk to the morgue felt like a death march to her own undoing. Terror surged through her veins, each step like walking on needles. The moment she saw her father's lifeless body, she vomited on the floor. Her husband lifted her gently, and with a silent nod, the staff began arrangements to create the death certificate.

Joviah was thrust into a new reality of responsibility. Since her father was unmarried, she was now responsible for making all the funeral arrangements.

Where should they bury him?

Did he have a will?

No.

"My father was very superstitious," she told them. "He believed that writing his will would summon the Angel of Death. The moment he signed it, he thought death would come for him."

"I tell you, Liberian people are fearless—except when it comes to death. They fear death, and even talking about it makes them feel like it might come for them. You can never ask a Liberian woman how many children she has. She'll always say,

'Enough.' If she gives you a number, her fear is that God will hear it, think she has too many, and take one away."

These old Liberian wives' tales had kept her out of a lot of danger—or maybe it was just her undiagnosed anxiety.

With the loss of her father, she felt like going back home would uncover things about him that she had never known. And that fear was almost too much to endure.

Henry looked at Joviah. "No matter what," he said gently, "I'm here by your side. We'll get through this together."

Kebbeh and James were still in the lobby when Jovi and Henry returned.

"Nah, mah, my dear," said Kebbeh. "Your father and I were together for many years. I'm so sorry."

James looked at Joviah, confused at what his mother had just confessed. He didn't know how to react. She had just lost her father, and now he was meeting the other sister she had never known existed.

A month later, the funeral was held in Michigan at St. Joseph's Catholic Church. Friends and relatives from Liberia and friends from his school days in America converged on the sleepy college town to pay respects—or to confirm that the boisterous, self-made Liberian banker had joined the ancestors.

The parishioners dressed in black. The family wore his favorite sky blue. Joviah brought the batik fabric from Fulton County and had a tailor make her funeral gown, his only child.

Between hymns of *Amazing Grace* and *Bread of Life*, whispers floated through the pews:

"Kebbeh is here, and she brought their child."

"Is James his son?"

When Joviah read her eulogy—scribbled on a first-class napkin during her flight from Paris—she thought of the songs he had once shared. Music had always been their love language.

"Songs are the soundtrack of our lives," she said. "Thank you, Daddy, for being my conductor. Your life's song will always give me solace and peace. I love you."

At the repast, the Silver Spring Banquet Hall was filled with poster boards and easels of his photos. As Joviah studied them, Beatrice muttered, "Don't quit your day job, my child. These posters look like a child made them."

Joviah froze, then laughed with her. "I know—they're awful. But I didn't expect Dad to die like this."

Aunties served Jollof rice, cassava leaf, and German chocolate cakes—his favorites. The DJ played Crystal Gayle, Bob Marley, The Staple Singers, Fifth Dimension, and Kenny G. Joviah wanted the room to celebrate his life.

But as the line of mourners blurred together, she wondered: Was this the same man who had doubted her choices? The same man who had begged her mother for a son?

In the ebb of silence, laughter, and tears, Beatrice spotted Kebbeh—also in sky blue, her head covered, her eyes red and swollen, the perfect look of a grieving widow.

"Kebbeh, what are you doing wearing his color? You are not family!" Gasps echoed through the room; forks and plates paused midair.

Kebbeh's face twisted in disgust. "Not family? I was his wife!"

Beatrice shouted back, "You two were never married. What makes you think you earned that color?"

Kebbeh's voice rose, unashamed and primal. "That man was the love of my life—and the father of my children!"

"You think you were the only woman that man was running behind?" shouted Beatrice. "You're a damn fool to think you were his only beloved."

Beatrice's fist clenched to fight, heart beating out of her chest. *"Don't let this stupid woman win. Don't let her spit on your years of pain and silence for your husband and your daughter's reputation."*

Kebbeh could feel the shame and embarrassment looking at the eyes of Joviah. She desperately wanted to explain her rights and prove to everyone there that she deserved to be his family. She desired vindication.

The mourners started to part like the Red Sea, afraid to see what was about to happen next, yet unable to look away from what was unfolding. Was Kebbeh going to reveal that Joviah and James were siblings, and she was their real mother? On the day they laid Boikai to rest? Was this her masterful plan after she saw Beatrice at the hospital the day he died?

In Michigan, there were no Liberian societal lines between the elite and the working class. Was she about to project her pain of losing her mother, Ma Eliza, and fulfill the powerful beating her mother wished she had delivered at the market when Beatrice humiliated her?

"Your mouth is going somewhere it doesn't belong, Kebbeh!" Beatrice snapped, her hands trembling as she pointed to the door across the room. "Get out of this place or, so help me God, I will pull that headtie off your dirty head to the ground!"

The hall erupted in whispers, chairs scraping, men trying to calm the situation. Uncles shouted in disdain, Aunties shook their heads in confirmation, remembering the day thirty-one years ago when they had gathered for Boikai and Beatrice's wedding. Now they watched in silence as the two women fought for his ghost.

"What the hell do you mean, children, Kebbeh?" Beatrice yelled.

The DJ killed the music. The only sound left was the exhausted breath of two women locked in grief and fury, standing on either side of the same dead man's legacy.

Kebbeh, now glaring at Beatrice, felt the weight of every eye in the hall fixed on her. She grabbed her son, James, and daughter, Ruby, and left the hall in tears.

Kebbeh's jaw tightened, her lips sealed in a thin line. *The truth was always mine—mine to keep and mine to curse.*

"Who needs Jerry Springer when you have the drama right here?" Henry muttered.

Joviah, mortified, rushed to her mother. "Did you really need to do that?! I've never been so embarrassed in my life!"

"You, of all people, Mother, want to save your face? Welp, that's over now."

Without drawing more attention, Joviah and Henry slipped out of the hall and onto the next flight to New York. All the while, a quiet certainty pressed in on her: it was time. Time to return to Liberia, to stand on the soil of her beginning, to face the hurt she carried, and to uncover what her life was meant to hold.

Six months later, in New York, she packed for the journey back—her father's ashes carefully sealed in an urn, ready to be carried home. That was when the courier arrived.

The envelope in his hands felt heavier than paper should. Joviah stared at the familiar handwriting on its surface, her pulse accelerating. She traced her father's script with her thumb, half expecting the ink to smear, half fearing it would scald her. For a long moment, she could not move, as if opening it would alter everything she thought she knew.

Finally, she turned it over. On the back, scrawled in her father's trembling hand, were just two words:

The Truth.

Chapter 12: Redemption

143

With breath, with eyes, with memories—we carry what is sacred. The Lone Star rises again, not in haste but in quiet triumph, reclaiming her excellence, one soul at a time. Rebuilding comes gently, small small, as we say. And sometimes, the fire must come—clearing what once was—so that new life may take root and bloom.

She held the envelope to her heart. The truth about her entire life was inside—"*The Truth.*" The weight of ultimate betrayal, from the two human beings God had assigned to guide her, pressed down, threatening to alter everything. Hands trembling, afraid to break the seal, she drew a deep breath and read aloud the final letter from her father.

"Dear Joviah,

I wished this did not have to come to pass of my death, to reveal my ultimate truth to you, my darling daughter. Please don't blame your mother; she is also a victim of our heartless lie. This letter is my Redemption Song. My death is the ultimate price for the ungodly selfishness that you did not deserve. Your mother, Beatrice, fell ill while giving birth. She had complications, and our baby boy was born asleep. I was so devastated by the child that we lost.

I had gotten the love of my life, Kebbeh, pregnant, right before I was married to your mother, and when she was giving birth, we discovered that she had twins. A boy and a girl. James Siaka came first, and you, my Joviah Nina, came last. Kebbeh made the ultimate sacrifice and gave you to Beatrice.

When Bea awoke to you on her chest, she thought you were hers all along. Our arrangement was to keep Kebbeh away from you because of how we got together and how we hurt your mother. This is my confession, and I am ready to face my consequences of what the Lord will order now that I am gone.

I urge you to reach out to your family. You have a wonderful brother who works hard, and a little sister, Rubilene Sandra. They also got my letter, and they are also in shock and bewilderment. This choice, Kebbeh and I made, was to give you the best life possible. Please don't take it out on your birth mother. She is so proud of the young woman that you have become. That last day of July 1980 was the best day and the saddest day of my life. Losing my son, I never got over it. I'm sorry that I compared his life, which never was, to your life. I know those years were painful, and I never took the time to explain why. I am gone, and I deeply regret that I will not be there to console you.

In God's Grace, Daddy.

The feeling of losing half of your existence, only to discover that the truth could undo you—it was a mind-altering torment she would not wish on her worst enemy. How do you keep living when the truth itself threatens to break you?

Joviah stared at her father's letter for a long moment, then fed it to the flames in her apartment fireplace. A single tear carved a line down her cheek as she reached for the only mother she had ever known.

"Joviah, your dad is finally at peace," Beatrice said, her voice calm, unshaken.

"You are my daughter. When you lay on my chest, you were mine—and you will always be mine. That will never change. God don't like ugly, but you must forgive your father. His burden is not yours to bear."

In Paris, James had read the same letter. Rage thundered through the apartment, football trophies shattering against the walls. His lover, Giselle, terrified, fled screaming. Heart hammering, James snatched his phone from his pocket and dialed his mother.

"You mean to tell me that man was my father all along? The man who treated me like I wasn't good enough because I chose football over college? While he sat in America, cheering for another family's child?"

His voice shook as he accused her. "How dare you keep this from me, Ma! I had a twin I never knew existed—for thirty years? No father came for me in the war. No father visited me in France. And now this? He was a coward—and so were you."

Kebbeh's reply was steady, cold. "Are you finished? It was not easy back then. Status was everything. He was married. Both families would have been destroyed if the truth came out. That was the cost. Now, go wash your face. Your sister is on her way from America. She will be in Paris tomorrow. I've arranged for you to meet."

James hung up, gutted. He knew he would never have closure. His few chances to confront the man he called "Uncle

Boikai" were gone. His father had taken the last word to the grave. James swore that his own future children would never suffer the same disgrace.

A week later, when Joviah met James in France, she felt as though a missing piece of her life had returned. Their mannerisms mirrored each other; even their laughter was the same. She saw herself reflected in him—the male version of her own stubborn determination. Both carried their father's fire—and his damage. This was an inheritance neither had asked for.

They vowed to return to Liberia on their thirty-first birthday, to stand on the soil where it all began. James hesitated, haunted by memories of a grandmother killed and a childhood stolen by war. But Joviah felt the pull of her roots in every fiber of her being. She had no memory of home, yet her spirit knew she had to return.

Six months later, on their golden birthday, the twins stood on the beach at Grand Coastal Mound, outside Monrovia, dressed in gold fabric Joviah had designed herself. The waves broke before them, timeless and relentless. The cool waters welcomed their feet—the children of the soil, finally home.

Joviah raised her face to the sun. "I stand in my truth. A warrior, bruised and tarnished, yet crowned. I refuse to live in lies. I choose to live now, with the days I have left."

James's eyes narrowed. "Days you have left? Joviah, what are you saying?"

"I'm sick, my brother," she whispered. "Before I left, they found a clot near my chest. The doctor forbade this trip, but I had to come. God assigned me to return home."

Panic seized him. "Then we go to the hospital, now! I beg you, mehn!"

She shook her head. "Come hell or high water, I needed to be here. Henry knows nothing can change my mind."

James's voice broke. "Gran-gran always warned me never to walk the beach alone. She said that's where our people disappear."

"That's not superstition," Joviah said softly. "That's historical trauma. But I am not afraid."

While James drifted toward a pickup football game with boys who recognized him, Joviah sat by the waves on a black boulder. The salt air mingled with the sweetness of oranges and monkey plums. Her grandmother's stories—the *Liberian Drummer Boy* book, the story of the orange vendor woman her mother recalled—were no longer tales but living truths.

In the distance, a stout elderly woman in bright indigo and ruffled pink lace walked toward her, lappa tied at her waist. Their eyes met.

"My child has returned," Ma Eliza said triumphantly. "The child I prayed plenty for."

A single tear slid down Joviah's cheek. They smiled at each other, hands clasped, warm sand pressing between their toes, the sun gilding their skin. Joviah whispered her final words: "Ubekwe Usewah. God is good."

And with that breath, Joviah left this earth.

Like her grandmother before her—the orange vendor woman—she too fulfilled her purpose. The orange blossom had returned: the child who was the precious gift of God.

Acknowledgments

Iam eternally grateful to God for guiding me through this life and for being ever present. Through Him, all things are possible.

I would like to thank my mother, Gbai, and my father, the late Emmett Metzger, for raising me and instilling in me the purpose of being unapologetically myself. Your love and legacy are the reasons this book came to fruition, and I am forever grateful.

To my stepfather, Stafford—thank you for your kindness and gentle spirit.

To my husband, Andy—thank you for your countless words of encouragement, your advice, and your thoughtful previews. I could not have done this without you. To my beautiful boys, Maxwell and Mateo—thank you for always keeping me on my toes and reminding your mama to "trust the process."

To my amazing sisters—Maima, Myatta, Mayem, and Emma—your love and light keep me going and inspire me to make you proud. To my sister, Missy—I truly appreciate you; your kindness, support, and heartfelt conversations are always treasured. To my wonderful in-laws, Mike and Liz—thank you for cheering me on through every step of this journey. To my big cousin, Madia—I'm so blessed and grateful for the bond we share. To my cousin-sister, Ngozi—thank you for always keeping it real and for your unwavering support. To my brothers-in-law—Dan, Ty're, Lewis, and Kyle—thank you for your support and your sense of humor.

To my person, Tara Jo—your wit, energy, and support mean the world to me. To my bestie-cousin, Maryann—thank you from the bottom of my heart, and "Fula's" too. To my sweet bestie, Bre—thank you for allowing me to share this new dream with you. To my Desert Rose Mastermind Group—your encouragement, space, and check-ins helped me write this book chapter by chapter. To my sweet "Kamoh" Jen—thank you for always being my courageous friend and confidante. And to Diana—thank you for that wonderful author retreat and for encouraging me to create my story.

To all of my Liberian family and friends—this book is my love letter to you. Every story, every laugh line etched on my face is a reflection of my devotion to you.

To my birthday club girls—Jenni, Lindsey, Sara, and Kristy—your encouragement and feedback have helped me immensely. To my nieces and nephews—thank you from the bottom of my heart for all your hugs and for reminding me that I can still chase my dreams.

To all of my family—the Yuohs, Metzgers, & Clarkes, you continue to make me feel that I truly belong.

To my 'twin' Kathy, thank you for cheering me on every step of the way. To my 'brother from another mother,' Dan, thank you for always encouraging me through and through.

Finally, to my phenomenal publisher, Heather—words cannot describe my gratitude for the opportunity to sign with Hezzie Mae Book Publishing. This journey with you has been nothing short of amazing, and your guidance has been superb.

About the Author

Jebeh Edmunds is the founder of Jebeh Cultural Consulting LLC, where she has led more than 70 organizations through cultural-competency training and inclusive workplace practices. An educator for 18 years, she brings her passion for storytelling to her podcast, *Cultural Curriculum Chat*, and her YouTube channel, *Mrs. Edmunds' Cultural Corner*. Drawing inspiration from  her Liberian heritage and the stories passed down through generations, Edmunds creates resources that uplift communities and foster understanding. Her debut novella, *The Orange Blossom* (Hezzie Mae Book Publishing, October 2025), explores identity, belonging, and intergenerational healing. She lives in Northern Minnesota with her husband Andy and two sons Maxwell & Mateo.

Connect with the Author

jebehedmunds.com

Facebook.com/jebehculturalconsulting

LinkedIn.com/in/jebeh-cultural-consulting

instagram.com/culturallyjebeh_

Leave a Review

If you enjoyed reading *The Orange Blossom*, would you consider leaving a review on a platform of your choice? Reviews help indie-published authors find more readers like you.

Continue the Journey

Thank you for reading *The Orange Blossom*. My hope is that this story spoke to your heart and opened new windows into the richness of Liberian culture and the power of resilience. The story doesn't end here- there are more ways for us to connect.

Visit my website **www.jebehedmunds.com** to explore lesson plans, cultural competency resources, and blog posts that inspire educators, leaders, and lifelong learners.

Listen to ***The Cultural Curriulum Chat*** podcast for conversation that sparks empathy, celebrate diversity, and empower communities.

Empower your learning. Enroll in on-demand mini and full courses to strengthen your cultural competency skills. Whether you're an educator, leader, or organization, there is a path for you.

Stay connected. Join my newsletter, ***The Inclusive Educator***, for updates, reflections, and special offers.

With gratitude,
Jebeh Edmunds